CHELSEA TATE

SERIES

COMEDY OF ERRORS

LISSA HALLS JOHNSON

PUBLISHING

Colorado Springs, Colorado

For Sue Brown,
who loved China first . . .
and always loved me and believed in me.

Our bizarre conversations gave me
the idea for this book. We always said,
"If someone was listening and didn't
know what we were talking about . . ."

COMEDY OF ERRORS

Copyright © 1995 by Lissa Halls Johnson.
All rights reserved. International copyright secured.

Library of Congress Cataloging-in-Publication Data applied for
Johnson, Lissa Halls, 1955–
     Comedy of errors / Lissa Halls Johnson.
         p.   cm. — (China Tate series ; 5)
     Summary: When China and Deedee overhear two writers at camp
talking about a book plot that includes murder, they imagine that a
real murder will occur.
     ISBN 1-56179-391-4
     [1. Camps—Fiction.   2. Imagination—Fiction.   3. Christian
life—Fiction.]   I. Title.   II. Series: Johnson, Lissa Halls, 1955–
China Tate series ; bk. 5.
PZ7.J63253Co   1995
[Fic]—dc20   95-17778
                                                                             CIP
                                                                              AC

Published by Focus on the Family Publishing,
Colorado Springs, Colorado 80995.
Distributed by Word Books, Dallas, Texas.

The author is represented by the literary agency of Alive
Communications, P.O. Box 49068, Colorado Springs, CO 80920.

This is a work of fiction, and any resemblance between the
characters in this book and real persons is coincidental.

Editor: Deena Davis
Cover Design: Jim Lebbad
Cover Illustration: Paul Casale

Printed in the United States of America
     95 96 97 98 99/10 9 8 7 6 5 4 3 2 1

I would like to extend special thanks to . . .

Marian Flandrick Bray, who wrote and directed
Little Red Writing Hood for the 1993 Mount Hermon Writer's
Conference and let me include portions in this book.

❧

Paul Nagy, whose wild ideas sparked my creativity
into a writing frenzy.

❧

Bill Myers, who taught me how to make a multi-layer cake.

CHAPTER ONE

"**T**ODAY IS IMAGINATION DAY," China Tate announced far too early in the morning for Deedee Kiersey. *Morning* was a bad word in Deedee's vocabulary.

"Today is the day we let our imaginations go wild!" China threw her arms out and her head back when she said "wild."

"Am I supposed to care?" Deedee asked, her voice husky and still full of sleep.

"Of course you care." China leaned over Deedee's face and Deedee plopped her pillow over her head. "It means we don't look at anything as normal today. Everything we do and say must be creative—exciting."

"As if Camp Crazy Bear hasn't been exciting enough this past month," came a muffled voice from under the pillow. "Staples, bears, freezers, atlaspheres, a way too famous person. I've had enough excitement. Boredom is beginning to look real appealing."

China sat on the edge of Deedee's bed and gently

1

bounced up and down. Deedee burrowed deeper into her covers.

"Come on, Deeds," China pleaded. "My mind needs exercise."

"Good. Go do calisthenics with the Marines. I'm trying to sleep here."

"But I can't imagine on my own. Imagining is only as good as those you share it with. And you're the best."

Deedee sighed and rolled over. She peeked out from underneath her pillow, her green eyes bleary and skeptical. "Why is this necessary so early in the morning?"

"It's necessary to keep our young, fertile adolescent minds from rotting."

Deedee groaned and rolled over. "My mind prefers rotting."

"Okay, revised edition. We'll start as soon as you wake up."

"If I ever do."

"I'll wait," China said cheerfully. She crawled onto the top of the bed and started to bounce harder and harder until Deedee's head jostled up and down with every bounce.

"China Jasmine Tate!" Deedee screamed. "I'm going to kill you!"

CHAPTER TWO

THE PLANE'S ENGINE SPUTTERED and crackled. "We're not going to make it, China," Deedee said, trying to keep the fear out of her voice.

"We'll make it," China insisted. "The plane won't, but we will. We have parachutes."

Deedee looked at her with round eyes. "We have one parachute, China. Only one."

China sighed and looked at Kemper, the director of the high school camp. He held what he called a safety rope in his massive hands. "Just jump," he said, sounding bored.

"We can't both jump," China told him. "We have only one parachute."

"You go," Deedee urged.

"No, you go," China replied. "You *must* go. You're wearing the special suit. If I jump, I'll fall and die. You'll jump and be saved."

"JUMP!" Kemper said, in his booming voice. "If you don't, I'll yank you off your feet."

3

"Goodbye, my sweet friend," Deedee said to China.

China hugged her and they linked pinkies.

Deedee turned away and ran down a long carpet. With a flying leap she landed on a trampoline that propelled her upward and forward. Then she stuck to the wall.

Deedee shrieked. China clapped. Kemper nodded his approval. "Cool" was all he said.

"How do I get down from here?" Deedee asked, her face smashed against the giant wall of Velcro.

Kemper held onto the rope attached to the climber's harness wrapped around Deedee's waist and legs. "Can't you push yourself off?"

Deedee tried pushing against the looped velvet Velcro wall. But the hooks all over her jumpsuit held her fast.

China trotted to the front of the room and stood on the mini trampoline. She tugged at Deedee's leg and it came away from the wall with a ripping sound. As soon as her leg was free she could push herself free. Deedee giggled. "This is so weird being stuck to a wall. Did you think of this one, Kemper?"

"No. Someone else did. I really don't have such a great imagination."

"My turn?" China asked.

"Not yet. I want to do it some more," Deedee said. "Besides you always get to do the fun things first."

"Because you're scared of them," China said.

"No I'm not," Deedee protested.

"Yes you are."

"Am not."

"Are too."

"Am not."

"Are too."

"D-too," Kemper said. "Star Wars. Ar-too and D-too need to quit fighting. I haven't got all morning, you know. I want to get this thing perfected before I have camp kids getting stuck to the Velcro wall."

"You high school camp directors are all alike," Deedee said in mock complaint.

"If you want to jump again, do it before I give it to your friend here," said Kemper.

"What'll we imagine this time?" Deedee asked China. "That the building is on fire? This imagining is actually more fun than I thought it would be."

"JUST JUMP!" Kemper boomed.

Deedee ran a little faster and jumped with a little more energy. She opened her arms and thumped against the wall. The air left her with an OOMPH!

"Are you okay?" China asked. Kemper looked as if he were taking mental notes.

"Yeff," came the muffled reply. "My mouff if fuhh uf Velcro fuff."

"I'll pull you down." China stood on the trampoline but could barely reach Deedee's shoe. "Can you push off at all?"

A few grunts came from above. "I don't thint so."

China turned to ask Kemper for help. He was wandering around, following Deedee's flight path with the safety rope trailing from his hands.

"Kemper. Can you quit muttering and come help me?" China asked.

Kemper trotted down the aisle and grabbed hold of Deedee's ankle.

"What are you guys doing?" came a voice from the back of the room.

"Hi, Dud!" Deedee said through her mushed mouth.

"Wait a minute!" Mr. Kiersey said, as he walked down the aisle toward them. He stopped halfway down. "I want to cherish this moment for a long time. My kid stuck to the wall. Can you get down, Deedee?"

"Uh-uh."

"Hmm," Mr. Kiersey said, rubbing his chin. "I might propose we get one of these for home. When Adam gets too rough, we'll just stick him on the wall."

Deedee started to shake with laughter. "Get me dooon."

"I'll loan you the Velcro suit," Kemper said. "Great stuff."

Mr. Kiersey checked his watch. "Better get her down. We've got an urgent situation over at Main Camp. The flu is spreading like wildfire through the staff over there. The kitchen is in desperate need of help. We're scrambling to find temporary replacements. As soon as one person gets better, another gets sick. We've got a revolving door of sick employees."

China sat on the trampoline. "What about Eela-puash?"

"The high school camp kitchen will do fine without

you for a week. Everyone will work an extra hour to cover for you."

Kemper lifted up on Deedee's leg. It ripped loudly, drowning out some of what Mr. Kiersey said. He continued speaking. "Along with the usual family camp, there's also going to be a small writers' conference going on at the same time. We've never had a writers' conference before. It ought to be interesting."

Deedee pulled her face away from the wall. "A riders' conference, Dad?"

Rip.

"Yes. A group of writers wanted a place to learn more about writing."

Rip.

"Can China and I go to any of the riding classes?"

"I'll have to ask the seminar director."

Deedee dropped to the trampoline and bounced a couple times. "What about the horses? Will we still be able to have access to the horses?"

"I don't see why not. As long as you do your job first. You'll have a couple hours off between meals. But you'll be putting in long hours, so don't expect much."

Deedee frowned. "You know I hate working in the kitchen, Dad."

"You'll survive."

China unhooked the carabiner from the back of Deedee's harness. Deedee unzipped the jumpsuit and stepped out of it.

Mr. Kiersey kissed his daughter on the top of her head. "Report to the main kitchen by eleven-thirty and talk to Rahja. He's expecting you."

Deedee made a face at her departing father. "How can I imagine that away, China?"

"Imagination is not supposed to make things go away, Deedee. It's supposed to make normal and yucky things more light and fun and creative."

"Thank you, Mother China."

China slipped into the jumpsuit. "I would love to attend your pity party, Deedee. Really I would. But right now I have some testing of the Velcro wall to perform before we have to brave the new frontier and culture of the main camp kitchen. So, if you wouldn't mind, please step aside and clear the runway for take-off."

China threw the safety line over her shoulder, eyed the trampoline, and willed her racing heart to quit being such a baby and stressing out over a little flight. She ran down the aisle. The instant her feet left the floor to jump once on the trampoline, she felt the safety rope tighten. The harness cinched up between her legs. One second she was flying, the next she was pinned to a wall. She pushed away, and with a slow rip, her body started to pivot like a door on hinges. Then the door slammed shut. There she was, stuck, with her back to the wall. She looked like she had been in the middle of a jumping jack and had frozen in time.

"Hey, China. Cool trick. You can come down now."

China tried shifting her weight. She tried pulling her arms away from the wall. But the more she tried to squirm, the less she was able to move.

"Okay, guys, you can get me down now."

Kemper looked at Deedee and winked. "Oh my! I'm late for a meeting."

Deedee looked at the clock on the wall. "Oh dear. I'm supposed to be in Main Camp."

"We'd better go," Kemper agreed.

And they took off.

China hung there in empty Sweet Pea Lodge. "Guys. Yoo-hoo! This isn't funny!" Her voice echoed in the large room. "Deedee! Kemper!"

There was no response. One of the screen doors along the side wall shuddered in a sudden breeze.

China smiled. *I guess I'll just pretend I'm a butterfly on display in a museum.*

CHAPTER THREE

"**I**'M NOT GOING TO WORK in the kitchen," Deedee told China after she had returned three minutes later to pull her from the Velcro wall.

"Yes, you are," China said, stepping out of the Velcro suit.

"I'm not," Deedee said, handing the suit to Kemper, who stood staring at the wall. "I hate working in the kitchen."

"You are going, and you'll find out how fun it is."

Both girls left Sweet Pea Lodge and began the walk over Deedee's shortcut to the main camp kitchen.

"I hate cleaning up other people's messes, China."

"Then, maybe you can work in the cooking part."

"I cook Cheerios and Lucky Charms. On a good day, peanut butter sandwiches, hot cocoa, and popcorn. That's as wild as I get."

"I'll be there," China said.

Deedee sighed. "I know, I know."

The girls walked through the forest in silence.

"We'll make it fun," China said softly.

"I hate it."

"Trust me."

"Uh-oh. Don't say those words."

"What words?"

"'Trust me.'"

"Why not?"

"Every time you say them, something crazy happens."

"It won't this time. Trust me." China skipped on ahead. "Remember, this is imagination day. Anything can happen."

"That's what I'm afraid of," Deedee muttered.

"What'd you say?" China spun around, pulling an almost invisible spider web from her mouth.

"Nothing."

"How much time do we have?"

Deedee looked at her plain black Swatch. "We have a few minutes."

"Okay, I want to show you something." China started to sit on a log bench next to the creek.

Deedee shook her head. She grabbed China's hand and pulled her off the path. They ducked between two trees and into a bush that seemed to have no entrance. Inside, the bush opened into a small cozy hollow. Two low, sturdy branches stretched across the dirt floor. Deedee sat on one, China on the other. Ivy crawled all around them. "Wow!" China said.

"I'd forgotten about this place," Deedee whispered. "I used to come here all last summer when I was mad at Mom and Dad . . . or sick of my brothers."

China closed her eyes. It smelled wonderful. Green and wet and fresh. The longer they sat quietly, the more they could hear little insects moving across leaves. Bigger creatures scurried unseen in the underbrush.

China opened her eyes. Shadows and light danced together on multicolored leaves. A brown spider dropped slowly in front of them.

"Look," China whispered. "It's Romeo leaving Juliet's balcony."

A smile took Deedee's face by surprise. "It's a parachuter," she said. "There's its plane," she said, pointing to a dragonfly flitting by.

"It's a window washer, washing the shaft of light."

"No, they're very tiny mimes pretending they're moving up an invisible wall."

"See how fun this is, Deedee?"

"Yeah."

"Look at that . . . ," China said, pointing to single strands of web stretching from one branch to another, glinting in the spotted sunlight.

Deedee pulled her massive curls back and nodded.

"It's a trail for Hansel and Gretel to find their way home."

"Nah," Deedee said. "It's a tightrope for a bug circus."

"A trip wire for fairies."

"We don't believe in fairies," Deedee said.

"Of course not. But when we imagine, we dream up stuff that can't necessarily happen. It's fun to think about. What if there *were* fairies? What if God made a community of small people who live out the Bible in a smaller way?"

Deedee had to ponder this. She bounced on her low tree branch.

China sighed. "We'd better go, even though I hate to leave this place."

Deedee led them back out into the bright sunlight. "Do we have to leave our imaginations in there?"

"No way! Now we're going to play, *Who Are Those People?*"

"I'm afraid to ask."

The girls ignored the bridge stretching across the raging creek and chose to cross over on a fallen pine tree. Deedee walked as if she were on a balance beam. China pretended she was escaping a madman.

Once across the creek, when they could hear each other again, China told Deedee the rules of the game. "One of us points out someone. The other one of us looks at the person and guesses where he or she is from and why the person is here."

"I can find out who they are by going through the registration roster."

"No fun. We want to guess."

"It doesn't sound like much fun to me."

The main camp lay dead ahead. People milled about the cars, taking out luggage. Kids ran helter-skelter, shrieking at the top of their lungs.

Deedee waved an arm across the crowd. "They're

all normal people, with normal lives who bring their wild children to camp for a week."

China whipped her head from side to side. "No, Dee-dee, no. See that pale white guy? He's a music teacher who never sees the light of day. Now look . . . coming out of the car next to him . . . see that Hispanic guy in white shorts? He's a world famous soccer player who's hiding out from autograph hounds."

As they moved through the parking lot, the girls smiled at the music teacher, the soccer player, and the screaming kids.

Deedee spoke up. "The kids are running around and screaming because they are locked up in city houses all day and can't go out to play."

"Boring. Too close to real life. They're inmates from a prison. This is their first day of freedom."

Deedee nodded her approval.

"Maybe the kids are planning on taking over the camp. Look, there's enough of them. They outnumber the adults by far."

Deedee laughed. "Maybe we should listen in. We might get some ideas."

As they passed the group of campers, China said out of the corner of her mouth, smiling all the while, "The guy with all the kids is a gynecologist."

"No, he's running an orphanage and these are all the poor orphans," Deedee whispered back.

"Now you're getting the idea," China said exuberantly. "That old guy . . ."

"The real old one?"

"Yeah, the short one who's bustling about. What about him?"

Deedee squinted her green eyes as if that would give her better vision into his soul. "He's that old guy in the movie about Peter Pan being all grown up. He's lost his marbles and he's looking for them."

"YES!" China smacked her hands together.

"Here he comes," Deedee warned.

"No, he's not. He's probably going to talk to someone behind us."

The old man walked briskly, his face gathered in jowls like that of an old sea captain. He stopped in front of the girls. "What're you lookin' at?" he growled.

The girls exchanged looks.

"You're spies, aren't ya? They think they're gettin' sneaky on me. But I know better. You just go tell your boss that Walter's on to 'em. They can't steal from me anymore. If they try, I'll give their little spies a taste of their own medicine. You understand?"

Deedee looked at China, then at the man. "Uh, yeah, I guess so."

"We're not spies," China said indignantly. "We're merely riders of the Old West."

Deedee's mouth dropped open. "China!"

"To earn our keep, we work in the chow hall."

The old man's eyes widened. "My specialty's the screen. The rough and tumble world of the Old West." His voice drifted off, his eyes narrowed. "You with the conference?"

"No," Deedee told him.

"But we intend to listen in and learn as much as possible," China said eagerly. "Maybe take away something we can use for ourselves."

Walter's scowly face pulled into itself again. "If you ain't with the conference, then stay away from me. I don't trust nobody no more. There are spies everywhere. They all steal from me. You best mind your own business."

Pushing between them, he walked away, his gait a hitch and a step.

Deedee let her breath out. "Wow! What do you make of him?"

"Someone must have let him out of the loony farm on a week-long pass."

"Do you think he's safe?"

"Probably harmless. He's got a better imagination than we do."

"What do you think he meant by us being spies and his specialty being the rough and tumble world of the Old West?"

China's eyes glazed over as she thought. Then, slowly, a smile took over her whole face. "Maybe he's with the riders' conference. He must be an old rodeo rider. Riding wild bulls. That's why he walks funny. He got thrown one too many times. The last time he landed on his head."

Deedee shook her head, laughing. "You're so much

better at this than I am. If I'm going to get better, I'd better practice every waking moment."

China smiled and gently yanked on Deedee's curls. "Fab! Okay. Look over there. See those two women?"

"The tall, big-boned one and the tiny one?"

"Yeah."

"They're obviously two friends who haven't seen each other in a long time," Deedee said.

China frowned. "No, Deedee!" she whined. "They're sisters who were separated by the tragic death of their parents. They haven't seen each other since they were four and seven."

"Wow!" Deedee said, staring at the embracing women.

The tall, big-boned woman wiped at her eyes. They stood and looked at each other without saying a word.

"How did they get back together again?" Deedee asked.

"They both signed up for camp on the same week. They didn't mean to; it was fate."

Both girls sighed, staring at the two women.

"But we don't believe in fate," Deedee said suddenly, breaking the bubble of happy fantasy.

"Of course not. It's just our imagination."

The bubble broken, they walked in silence to the kitchen.

"And what will the kitchen be?" Deedee asked, as the hot food smells accosted them before they reached it.

"It could be a prison dungeon where we have to

work off some dastardly deed we have done. But then we'd hate working there."

Deedee put her hand on China's arm, stopping her. "I really don't want to work in there. Not even if we do make up some story to make it easier."

"Grow up and deal with it. You'll get over it. It's not that bad." China smiled a fake comforting grin.

"Oh, thanks."

"What would make you happy?" China asked her, moving slowly up the hill toward the kitchen's back door, where steam poured out as if something were on fire.

Deedee closed her eyes and a soft smile came over her face. "I know. This is a royal palace. Only the best food and drink are served here."

"Boy, is that a stretch . . ."

Deedee's eyes flew open. "Be quiet. I'm trying to imagine." She closed them again and the soft smile returned. "We are princesses in the royal palace. Unrecognized. A jealous and wicked midwife stole us at birth and switched us with her daughters. But since we truly are the *wonderful* and *good* princesses, we are willing to work hard to serve our wonderful subjects until the truth is discovered."

"Whoa! Your mind can really go when it wants to," China said with approval.

Deedee opened the screen door and stepped into the kitchen. China followed, expecting another kitchen like Eelapuash. What she saw made her fall back a step. All around her, gadgets and appliances of stainless steel loomed like giant insects ready to devour their prey. Warmers and ovens, tables, industrial-size cans of food, people, steam, and attitude. Lots of attitude. But not like those happy, carefree ones in Eelapuash. Here it seemed more like a busy hospital emergency room. Solemn faces. People intent on tasks. No one paying attention to the newcomers.

Without thinking, China linked pinkies with Deedee. The two stood, thinking ahead to their week-long sentence.

"We *are* princesses," Deedee said, as if trying to convince herself. "Right?"

After Eelapuash, China never thought she'd feel intimidated by a kitchen again. But this one chased that foolish idea far away into the forest of reality.

A Middle Eastern man approached them, his movements quick and determined. He gave a little bow. "Hello, Deedee, and . . ."

"Hi, Rahja," Deedee said. "This is China."

"Ahh, good," he said, bowing a little again. "I am pleased to have your help. We are busy, as you can see. With not enough help and too many people falling to the sickness all the time. I do my best. But I need help."

"We're happy to serve," China said softly.

"Come, please."

Rahja led them to a huge cauldron. A girl about eighteen years old stirred the steaming, bubbling brew with a giant whisk. She seemed to be stewing as much as the brew.

China's eyes grew wide. *It's like our fantasy really coming to life. Is this the wicked midwife?*

Rahja spoke. "Glenda, these are the two girls I said were to come help."

There's really a person named Glenda?

Glenda's eyes flashed. "You mean the girls who are to replace Lori."

Rahja shrugged. "This is China. And this is Deedee. They will help you any way they can. You will need to give them a tour of both upstairs and downstairs." And then he disappeared into the bowels of the kitchen.

Glenda glared at the girls. "I don't want you here, you know."

"Why not?" Deedee asked, astounded.

China knew Deedee wasn't used to being unwanted anywhere in Camp Crazy Bear. When your dad is the camp director, everyone is nice to you.

"I think you know," she said, practically spitting the words. She spun around and faced her cauldron. With one arm she wiped the sweat off her brow.

China and Deedee stared at each other. *"It's happening,"* Deedee mouthed to China.

China nodded in response. *It's really happening.*

CHAPTER FOUR

GLENDA GAVE THEM a whirlwind tour of the kitchen, during which China learned nothing. She assumed that's what Glenda hoped she'd learn. Maintaining her nasty attitude, Glenda put the girls to work stirring the steaming soup, then ladling it into a bizillion bowls for lunch. As the family campers trooped into the dining hall for their first meal, Glenda peeked through the swinging doors at the small group of adults clustered around tables a short distance away from the main family conference.

"These writers are weird people," Glenda said. A kitchen worker entering through the squeaky swinging door distorted some of what she said.

"I think riders are cool," China told her. "I'd be a rider, too, if I had time."

"It figures," Glenda snorted. "If you like them so much, you can wait on them."

China thought fast. She figured Glenda only wanted to torture them, so she put on a fake, whiny voice.

"Oh, please don't make us wait on tables."

Deedee picked up the idea. "I *hate* waiting tables," she muttered in false misery.

"Well, isn't that too bad?" Glenda said. "Rahja told me to assign work for you both, and that's your assignment."

"Only the wicked midwife and her daughters could be so cruel," China moaned.

"What are you talking about?" Glenda asked. She shook her head. "Never mind, I don't want to know. You guys are weird. You'll be perfect out there with that loony bunch."

The writing group sat at ten round tables of eight people each. All of them had blue notebooks with a white-rearing stallion on the front. The reference to a verse was written in an Arabic style-calligraphy in the lower right corner.

China's and Deedee's job was to carry food out to the tables and watch for empty dishes and inquiring faces.

After the prayer for the opening meal was said by Mr. Kiersey, China and Deedee left the kitchen with steaming bowls of soup. They repeated the trip until each table had soup, bread, and relish tray, and, had been encouraged to visit the well-stocked salad bar.

"Have you noticed?" Deedee said to China during one refill trip into the kitchen. "They seem to gossip an awful lot."

China shrugged, nibbling on a carrot stick. "I thought

it was more like telling stories. You know, like cowboys do. Didn't they all tell stories about the Old West while sitting around the campfire? Maybe mealtime is a rider's time to tell stories."

Deedee smiled. "Makes sense to me." She picked up a refilled bowl of soup and disappeared through the swinging door.

China moved slowly around her tables, trying to hear what the people were saying without looking too intrusive.

Most of the conferees seemed to talk to everyone at the table around them, but the two women the girls had decided were long-lost sisters talked only to each other, a seeming conspiracy between them.

"They're trying to decide what to do about the evil woman who separated them," China told Deedee.

"I would swear they're up to no good," Deedee said, pondering the situation.

"Get to work!" Glenda growled.

All through lunch, China tried to smile at Walter, but he kept glowering at her and muttered something about Hollywood and her being a spy. She wanted to pat him on the shoulder and reassure him. Or give him a hug and take him home for coffee and doughnuts. She figured he could be a marvelous replacement for her absent grandfather. But Walter was building a huge invisible brick wall between them for reasons China couldn't fathom. She chalked it up to too many falls off wildly contorting bulls.

As the girls began to clean off the tables, Rahja rushed out to them. "Deedee, China, I have a very urgent message for you. Samuel J. Gleckenspiel from Warner Brothers Studios called on the phone to speak with you. He's a producer. Has an important question for you."

Deedee and China exchanged questioning expressions. They knew this had to be the work of B.T., who was the star of a television series. He had recently come to the camp for a week, and he and China and Deedee had become good friends.

Walter's expression perked up and grew darker at the same time.

"Where can we call him back?" Deedee asked.

"He wouldn't give me the number. Said the number is confidential. He was very busy and would get back to you."

"When? Where?" China asked eagerly.

Rahja stuck his chin a little higher into the air. "I tell him you girls work hard here. You are not at his whimsical desires."

Deedee's face fell. "What did he say?"

"He say he call you on your break. 3 P.M. Phone near infirmary. He has phone number."

Deedee checked her watch.

"Did you give him the phone number?" China asked, confused at how a Hollywood producer could get that number. Or how B.T. could have gotten it, for that matter.

"No. He have it. He call. You be there." Rahja looked sternly at them, his eyes narrowing. "But you work hard or you have no break."

Walter had opened his blue notebook and scribbled in it. He pushed back his chair and scurried away.

At 3:00 sharp, the girls were at the phone by the infirmary. They linked pinkies, then let go.

"What do you think?" China asked for the hundredth time. "What's B.T. up to now?"

Deedee looked exasperated. "We're about to find out, okay?"

At 3:15, the phone still hadn't rung. A small figure hobbled around through the shadows, trying to be obscure and not succeeding.

"What do you think Walter is doing?" Deedee asked.

"Who knows? He seems to be obsessed with Hollywood. Don't let it bug you."

The phone rang, jarring them to life. "You answer," China said to Deedee.

"No, you," Deedee said.

"You're the one who can talk to anyone about anything. I freeze up. You answer. Just pretend it's someone interested in Camp Crazy Bear."

Deedee straightened her lanky frame and held her chin up. "Hello, this is Miss Deedee Kiersey. How may I help you?" China leaned her head against Deedee's so she could hear the conversation.

"Miss Kiersey," came a nasal-sounding voice over the phone. "Let me introduce myself. I am Mr. Samuel J. Gleckenspiel, the president and CEO of Warner Brothers's Idea Department. And I have it under good authority that you might be able to feed us some marvelous leads for ideas."

Deedee pushed her lips together, rolling her eyes at China. She put her hand over the mouthpiece. "It's B.T. What a weirdo."

"Play up to him," China whispered back. "Remember, today is imagination day. Let's imagine to the max."

A slow smile crept over Deedee's mouth, spreading to her green eyes. "Why, Mr. Gleckenspiel," she said in a loud, authoritative voice. "I am highly honored. I and my partner, Miss China Jasmine Tate, would be happy to assist you in any way possible. What kind of ideas are you looking for?"

Walter had stopped pacing in the shadows and inched closer to the girls. Whenever they looked his direction, he quickly looked down at his open notebook, pretending to study its pages.

"Camp stories. Funny stories. Incidents. Anything that would make a good television series. We're looking for new series ideas for next season."

"Ideas for series," Deedee said, as if writing it down. "What about suspense or fantasy kinds of ideas?" Deedee asked.

China whispered into Deedee's ear. "Does he really think we're falling for this?"

Deedee shrugged.

"Anything, anything. We'll pay you well."

"How well will you pay us?" Deedee asked, her voice taking on a very professional tone.

"How about ten thou per?"

China choked.

"It's only pretend," Deedee reminded her. Then, to the phone, Deedee said, "How will we get these ideas to you?"

"I'll call every day at three-fifteen. Do you think you know what to do?"

Deedee looked over at Walter, who now glared at them. "Yes, we know what to do," she said, still looking at Walter.

A mighty storm of emotion spread over Walter's face. The phrase, "If looks could kill," came to China's mind. She shuddered, then pushed the irrational fear away.

Deedee put the phone back in its cradle and the two girls started to howl with laughter. Then they composed themselves.

"Well, Deeds, my dear partner," China said. "I do believe it is time for us to go into the idea business."

Deedee linked her arm through China's. "I do believe you are correct."

Walter scurried away as they approached, muttering like the distant roll of thunder.

Deedee dropped her head back, her Spanish-tile curls baking in the sun. "Can you imagine this if it were real? If we really could get paid for coming up with ideas?"

"Okay," China said happily. "We can imagine it all the way back to work."

CHAPTER FIVE

THE NEXT MORNING, the sun bleached the blue right out of the sky. The still air hung hot and heavy.

"We're in God's great industrial oven," China intoned, "being baked for some giant heavenly party."

Deedee wiped her hand across her forehead. "Gingerbread girls?"

China nodded, her head feeling like it had gained an extra ten pounds overnight. "I just hope God doesn't forget and overbake us."

"I don't suppose the castle kitchen will be much cooler," Deedee said.

"Probably not." China moved her arms against her body, hoping her T-shirt would catch the drips of sweat trickling down her sides. "Do we have enough time to cool off before we go to work?"

Checking her watch, Deedee smiled. "If we time it right, we could have ten minutes."

China used the rest of her flagging energy to trot to the creek. The water looked so inviting, she plopped herself down into it. "Auuhhh!" she cried immediately, standing up. "The water is freezing!"

"China! You can't go to work sopping wet," Deedee said, wading knee-high into the creek.

"In this heat, it'll probably take about thirty seconds to dry off." China sat back down, putting her hands into the water, the current tugging them. "Look!" China said, watching them bob. "If they weren't attached, they'd be gone."

"If your head wasn't attached, you'd let that go too." Deedee looked at her watch again. "Come on, China, you'd better get out or your clothes won't dry off in time."

"Such a worrier. You'll make a marvelous mother." China stood, looking around. "Where's your hideout? That would make a great spot to dry off without getting heatstroke in the process."

Deedee splashed some water on her arms and face. "Over here." She tromped out of the creek and within moments had once again made a door where there was none in the middle of trees and bushes that looked no different than everything else around them. "Seven minutes," she told China, as she relaxed on a low, springy tree branch.

China sat across from her and closed her eyes. In the shaded shelter, drenched from the waist down, she felt she was in an air-conditioned room. "Umm, this feels wonderful. Maybe we should call in sick today. I don't think princesses should have to work. There must be a law against it somewhere."

"How I wish that were true, China dear."

"Shh," China said, cocking her head as if to hear better. "Someone's coming."

Deedee peered through the bushes. "It's those ladies. The long-lost sisters." Then she put her finger to her lips.

The women sat on the fallen log right outside the girls' hiding place.

"Oh great! Trapped," China mouthed to Deedee. Deedee rolled her eyes.

"You know, Marjean," the small woman began. "I'm going to have to kill Harrison."

"Kill?" Deedee mouthed. *"She can't mean it."*

"NO!" the large woman said. "Belina, I thought you loved Harrison. Every time you talk about him your voice gets all mushy. If I didn't know better, I'd swear you loved him enough to marry him."

China glanced at Belina's ring finger. A large diamond ring sparkled there. *"She's already married!"* She mouthed to Deedee. Deedee frowned and shook her head in disgust.

"I do love him. Very much. He's more real, more solid than any other character I've ever . . ."

"He is! So why are you going to kill him?"

"I have to. He simply has to go. He knows too much. The others know he knows everything."

"What's really sad is that, for all intents and purposes, Harrison doesn't exist. No records of his birth. No work records. No medical records. Nothing."

Belina chewed on her cheek as she thought. "Cults are known to do that. I really wanted Harrison to escape. But I didn't think his escape would force him to be murdered."

Tears formed in Belina's eyes. "His parents did such a great job of concealing his existence that, once he's gone, no one will miss him. No one will know he is dead. No one will mourn his passing. Isn't it sad to have this great person, and when he dies, he won't be remembered by anyone?"

"Except you."

"It's hard for me to believe he has to die. But I know he does."

"Belina, please. Can't you change that?"

"I've tried. I've really tried. But it's gone too far for that. I would have to redo the whole thing and there's no time. I've hoped I could change some little things in order to make a difference, but I can't. Marjean, there's no other way."

China looked at Deedee, her eyes reflecting a mixture of fear and shock. They couldn't leave now, even if there had been a way for them to escape unseen.

"Have you talked to your agent?"

"Yeah. But he said that's what the big boss says has to be done. There's not much he can do at this point either."

Marjean shook her head. "Sometimes they can be far too intrusive, you know? I think you ought to be able to do what you want with whom you want."

Belina put her chin in her hands, staring at the

rushing creek. "When you sign a contract and they pay you the big bucks, you do what they say."

"Is she a hit man? Is this the Mafia?" Deedee mouthed. China shrugged in response and put her finger to her lips.

Marjean sighed. "I guess. I'm just glad I'm working with kids. No one tells me to kill anyone. Actually, I'm not allowed to, even if I wanted."

Both women chuckled. China and Deedee looked at each other, appalled. *"How can they laugh about killing kids?"* Deedee mouthed.

"They're totally sick," China responded.

"So when does it have to be done?" Marjean asked.

"By Friday."

"Whew! That soon."

"They have schedules to keep. Deadlines to meet."

Marjean shook her head. "When do you think you'll do it?"

"I'm not sure. Our schedule is so busy here. I'll need your help. I'm not real good at this."

"I'll help any way I can, you know that."

"Thanks, Marjean. I appreciate you so much."

The women hugged briefly, then Belina looked at her watch. "Our seminar has already started. We'd better hurry."

The girls stared at each other. China could have been looking into a mirror of her own face when she looked at Deedee: dropped jaw, wide open eyes, a frozen expression of horror. China's heart pounded in her chest. "What'll we do?" she whispered.

Deedee peered out the bushes once more. Her unseeing eyes darted back and forth as if she were trying to figure out the solution in her mind. "We've got to stop them."

China looked out the bushes too, her heart still pounding, the sweat dripping from fear now, rather than heat. "How?"

"We tell the cops."

China shook her head. "I think we need more proof. If we tell the cops now, they probably wouldn't believe us. And then, what would we have? Even if they did believe us, and if they questioned the women, do you think they would 'fess up?"

Deedee snorted. "Not those two. They're as cold as ice."

"As cold as a glacier," China corrected.

Deedee looked at her watch. "We'd better jet to work. During our break we can see if there's a Harrison registered here this week. If not, I don't know how they'd kill someone long distance."

China nodded. Without a word, the girls moved out of the thicket and ran the whole way to the kitchen.

The kitchen, unfortunately, hadn't changed in the few short hours China and Deedee had been away from it. It still had a sort of organized chaotic look about it. Glenda still snarled at them and gave them the tasks she obviously detested. China didn't mind the tasks so much, it just didn't seem right that she and Deedee had to sliver crates of lettuce heads when a murder was imminent. She went over in her mind all the reasons why they should call the police and all the reasons why they shouldn't.

If they called the police, they could keep poor Harrison from meeting his horrible fate. But that was only if they knew who he was. If he had no identity, then the police couldn't track him. Would the police really believe a couple of fifteen-year-old girls? They were probably all like Dr. Hamilton, who didn't believe teenagers were human. If they did call the police, they would be asked too many questions they couldn't answer. And really, what could they say? That they had overheard two sweet Christian women plotting a murder? Who would believe them? No, the best idea was to simply do as much listening and investigating as they could.

China wanted so badly to ask Deedee what she thought, but people moved around them constantly in the kitchen. People who might overhear them and ask questions. They had to avoid questions until they knew more of the answers.

"You wait on the table where the ladies are sitting," Deedee whispered to China, as her father made announcements to the group. "Try and hear everything you can."

"Okay. You wait on the one next to it and we'll stagger our trips out there. That way we can hear more."

Deedee nodded, then bowed her head for the prayer.

Serving the "riders" tacos for lunch took more energy than China could have imagined. They wanted refills of everything before the serving dishes had gone once around the table.

"Why can't we just put more on each serving dish?" Deedee asked Glenda.

"Because," Glenda snapped, "we never know how much they will eat of one thing. State health laws require we throw out everything left on the serving platter. We can't afford to waste too much food."

China noticed that other servers did not have to hustle back and forth so much between the kitchen and tables. Either the "riders" were hungrier than the families, or Glenda was simply being the "mean midwife" again, trying to make more work for the "poor little princesses" trapped in their castle kitchen.

China hated having to work so quickly. She could only duck in and out of the conversation between Belina and Marjean. This time the two women talked a lot with the people at their table.

By mid-meal, China could stand it no longer. She moved herself between the two women, slowly setting down the fourth refill of platters onto the table.

". . . go riding with me tomorrow . . ."

"I haven't the time, Marjean. I've really got to figure out how I'm going to do this," Belina told her, while delicately dropping meat into her taco shell.

"Maybe riding will give you some ideas of what to do. I'll help you brainstorm." Marjean took the meat bowl and ladled some onto her plate. She then looked up at China, who had frozen as if she were suddenly invisible. "Can I help you?" Marjean asked her.

China blushed, then recovered. She announced loudly to the whole table, "Is there anything else I can get for you?"

Some people shook their heads; a couple said, "No, thank you." China turned away, hoping the women didn't think anything of her blunder.

China returned to the back of the dining hall, watching her tables for a sign they needed something else. She watched Deedee bend her head toward Walter, pull away quizzically, then leave the table with her brows furrowed, her eyes scanning the ground as if searching for something. China moved next to her for the return trip to the kitchen.

Deedee looked up, startled to see China. She looked over her shoulder at Walter, then back at China. She jerked her head toward the kitchen door and China followed her.

"What's going on?" China asked.

"I wish I knew," Deedee said, putting down her empty bowl and platter. "Walter beckoned to me and said, 'You touch mine and I swear you'll have no future.'"

"What's that supposed to mean?"

"I don't know. I'm trying to figure it out."

"You didn't ask him?"

"It threw me. I didn't know what to say."

China peered through the window in the swinging kitchen door. "Maybe he's just an old man, not quite in touch with reality any more. My grandfather is starting to get like that. Sometimes he gets mad about things that happened years ago. It's like his mind is slipping into the past. A few minutes later he's fine again."

"Maybe you're right. I'd better get these refills out there."

CHAPTER SIX

AFTER LUNCH, GLENDA SENT China and Deedee to the pit. Warm, moist air greeted them as they walked down the rubber-matted, dank stairs.

"What's down here?" China asked. "A torture chamber?"

"Might as well be," Deedee sighed. "The people assigned to the pit spend hours washing dishes."

"That's not so bad," China said. "Now maybe we can talk."

Dishes literally came into the pit by the truckload, since the outlying children's camps sent in all their dishes too. The dishes that didn't come in by truck came in by the dumbwaiter, a small elevator that transported loads of dishes from the kitchen upstairs to the pit below. The cement floor had several drains sunken into it. Thick rubber mats with giant holes in them lay about like sinking rafts in the middle of a water flow.

"This place is trippy," China said to Deedee. Soap

suds swept past them in a frothy river as they stepped from mat to mat.

A man, looking more like a stick person than a real one, introduced himself in a thick English accent as Nigel. "I'm so glad to have you here. With everyone sick, it's hard to run Huge Harold all by myself." He waved his hand at a monstrous dishwasher. It made the small machine China used in Eelapuash look like a doll house model. She walked around Huge Harold, her mouth gaping. Harold hissed and churned and grunted continuously. It seemed Huge Harold was a stomach that was never satisfied, always looking for more to devour.

Nigel set a crate of dishes on top of a table next to Huge Harold. "Set them in like so, and then throw the crate in after it."

It was easy to run. Giant plastic teeth ran on a conveyor belt through the metal belly where the dishes were washed, sanitized, and rinsed—all in a matter of five minutes. They came out the other side steaming, drying before they reached the end of the conveyor belt.

China and Deedee set the plates on their sides between teeth without even rinsing them first. Silverware, after being sanitized and soaked in the same blue solution China used at the high school camp kitchen, were put into crates that kept them standing on end and separated for a secondary cleaning process.

After the girls got the rhythm down, they began to relax and talk, the hungry noises of Huge Harold drowning out their conversation to anyone's ears but their own.

"Maybe we should just forget this," Deedee said. "We could tell Dad . . ." She closed her mouth on her words, then smiled weakly at China. "Sorry. I forgot."

"But what about Harrison? Is that fair to him?"

"What can we do, China? We're just a couple of kids who overheard something we shouldn't."

"I say we follow them," China retorted.

"Follow them?"

"Spy on them. See what else they are doing. What they said at lunch proves Belina doesn't know when or how she's going to kill him yet. They're going to talk about it tomorrow while on a horseback ride. We could go on the ride with them. Maybe we could get more ideas then."

Deedee sighed as she lifted another blue crate onto the table. "I suppose the least we can do is find out if anyone named Harrison is registered at camp."

"And if there is, we can tell your dad then."

"Now, we just have to figure out when to get to the records. They always have them under lock and key. The whole privacy thing, you know? Dad once told me they even have people who come to camp to sort of hide out. Maybe Harrison is doing that."

"When can we get to the records?"

"It will have to be after dark. No one is allowed in

there except two secretaries. If we get caught, I bet
we'd be in more trouble than we ever dreamed."

Promptly at 3:15, the phone by the infirmary rang.
"Samuel J. Gleckenspiel here," the nasally voice said.
"Have any ideas for me yet?"

China spoke into the phone. "We are following a
very important lead."

"Give me the gist of it," Mr. Gleckenspiel suggested.

"No, it has to do with some of the people here. We
can't let them know that. They would be awfully mad
and might harm us." China laughed quietly. *B.T. is so
weird.*

"Oh, yes, I see," Mr. Gleckenspiel responded.

China thought she saw an elbow belonging to
Walter pop out from behind a tree. It seemed to be
moving frantically, as if the hand attached to it were
writing something important.

"One warning, Miss Tate. Whatever you do, do not,
I repeat, do NOT speak to the *Star World Enterprise*
tabloid if they should call regarding your interlude
with Mr. Brian Thomas last week. They are looking
for any story they can get on him. They will be nice
and offer lots of money. But do not trust them!" The
phone went dead.

Deedee frowned. "B.T. is so good, I forgot it was
him. And I wanted to talk to him."

China smiled and patted her on the back. "He wants
to play this game for some reason. Let's give him the
benefit of the doubt."

That night after dinner, the girls told Mrs. Kiersey they wanted to take a walk. As they opened the door to leave, the phone rang. After Mrs. Kiersey answered, she called to them, "Wait! It's for you!"

Deedee took the phone from her mom. After listening for about two seconds, she screamed. "B.T.!" Then she looked at her mother. "Mom, can I get on the extension in your room?"

Mrs. Kiersey nodded. China picked up the fallen receiver and held her breath, trying to calm the feelings tumbling inside her. B.T. was her best friend besides Deedee. But then, maybe he didn't feel that way any more. Then again . . .

"B.T.?"

"China! Did you lose Deedee?"

"She'll be on in a sec. Hey, B.T., what's with the phone calls in the afternoon?"

Deedee picked up the extension.

"What phone calls?" B.T. asked.

"You'd make a great Hollywood producer," Deedee said. "Great voice for it."

"Thanks, but what does that have to do with phone calls?" B.T. asked.

China wished Deedee were standing there in the room with her. She needed to see what Deedee thought. Was B.T. telling the truth? Just being silly? It was hard to tell. There was something hovering on the edge of his voice.

"Samuel J. Gleckenspiel," China said.

"How do you know that name?" B.T. said. "You're confusing me."

"Mr. Gleckenspiel, we have an idea for you," Deedee said in a funny voice.

"I'm still confused."

"Why are you calling us and pretending to be a producer?" Deedee said bluntly.

"I'm not calling and pretending to be anybody. I'm calling you now to see what's up. See how you're doing."

"You aren't calling us in the afternoon?" China asked skeptically.

"Nooo . . ." B.T. said slowly. After a moment of silence, his voice came on the line again. "Someone saying he's Mr. Gleckenspiel is calling you?"

"He said he's a producer for Warner Brothers," China told him.

"But we figured it was you," Deedee said.

"Not this time."

"Then who . . . ?"

"There's this guy at work," B.T. continued. "He asked about my week at camp, and I told him. He thought the Atlasphere thing was pretty funny and said he might like to do a series about a summer camp. I told him you guys would be the ones to talk to. Maybe he took me seriously."

"Is he really a producer?"

"Yeah. He does all the favorite Friday night shows. Sit-coms, all of them. Mine's in that line-up. They're always looking for new shows to launch."

China sat on the floor and twirled the curly phone cord over her fingers. She tried to decide if B.T. was telling the truth or playing one of his characters again.

Deedee, she decided, must be having the same problem. There was a moment of silence before she blurted, "We're working at the main camp kitchen this week."

Mrs. Kiersey came up behind China. "I'm sorry, girls. But I'm expecting an important phone call. Can you talk to B.T. another time?"

The girls reluctantly said their goodbyes to B.T. and left the house quietly.

"Do you think it's him?"

"I don't know," China said. "I figure it probably is. What producer would really call us and care about what we think?"

Deedee's head bobbed. "Yeah. That's how I feel."

China sighed. "I wish B.T. were here to help us."

"If he was, we'd be laughing instead of stressing out."

China smiled at the thought. "At least we've got something to look forward to every day. A laugh in the middle of something terrible."

They crossed the creek in silence. Minutes beyond dusk, only a sliver of moon hung low in the pale sky. China shivered. "What if we get caught breaking into the file room?" she whispered.

"I don't know," Deedee answered with a shiver of her own.

"I'd probably be sent back to Aunt Liddy." That brought a deeper shiver.

"Probably."

"And you?"

Deedee bit her lip and pushed at her curls. "I don't know. I don't want to think about it. One thing's for sure. We'd be in major trouble."

Deedee looked around, watching for something, but she didn't know what.

The administration building lay before them like a dark sleeping millipede, its legs the white painted lines waiting for cars to park between them.

"Maybe we shouldn't do this," Deedee suggested.

"We are Harrison's only hope. Look. We helped Bologna and things turned out okay there."

"Deedee!" A deep voice came from behind them.

China thought she'd lost her heart somewhere down around her knees. The man behind them was dressed in a light green shirt with a security patch on his arm. A flashlight lit the way before him, swinging from side to side with each step.

Deedee gave him a weak smile. "Mr. Gibbons. Hello."

"Another fine evening."

"Yeah. Me and China are just out for a walk."

"I never worry about you, Deedee. It's nice to know I can trust you to do what's right."

Deedee's forced smile didn't change. China was aware of every breath she took, as if her breathing would give away her thoughts.

"Have a pleasant evening!" Mr. Gibbons moved away, the light leading him into the darkness.

Deedee exhaled as if she had been holding it. "Come on," she said, "Let's do it now or not at all." She took a few steps, then stopped. "Wait a minute! What a ninny I am! No one suspects me of doing anything wrong, so if we walk into the building like we belong, it's no big deal. I go in and get stuff for my dad all the time."

"But if someone sees us go in and reports us . . ."

"I'm not saying we don't have to sneak in . . . but we don't have to walk around the grounds like criminals. We're not criminals. Those ladies are."

"Women," China corrected. "They don't sound like ladies to me."

Deedee used a key to open the back door. Once inside the building, she led China through a maze of hallways.

"At least the file room doesn't have any windows. Come on."

She opened a door and started down a pitch-black staircase. China followed. At the bottom Deedee whispered, "Wait here." She opened another door with a key and quickly turned on the light and punched in a series of numbers into the alarm key pad on the wall. "Let's do it."

She led China into a large room and closed the door behind them. File cabinets lined the walls. She walked toward the back wall, opened a drawer, and removed three file folders. "This week's registrants." She put the folders on a work table in the middle of the room. China took one and immediately started to flip through the papers. Deedee took another and did the same.

"Harrison, Harrison, Harrison," muttered China as she looked at name after name. *First name. Last name. Any name.*

Deedee read more slowly. Her lips moved, reading each name silently.

China finished the first file and reached for the third. "Come on, Harrison. Please be here." She opened the file and read the top paper. "Deedee. You have the wrong file. This is an employee's file."

Deedee stopped, standing upright. "Shh. I think I hear something."

China froze.

Deedee moved silently toward the door and stuck one eye up to the peephole. She turned to look at China. "Someone's coming. With a flashlight."

China's heart again fell to her knees and she swallowed hard.

CHAPTER SEVEN

DEEDEE SNAPPED OFF THE LIGHT and the girls hid under the table. Only then did Deedee realize she had not closed the door tightly. The door opened with no more noise than a soft swish.

The flashlight moved around the room. China closed her eyes and held her breath. When she opened them, she watched feet move around the table. But they weren't the shoes of the security guard. They were worn-out white tennis shoes below a pair of ankle-tight blue jeans. She nudged Deedee and pointed. Deedee's eyes grew wide.

A file drawer opened and they could hear the sound of files being rifled. "Oh, mustard!" came a slightly familiar voice. "Where is it?" The feet moved around the table and the overhead light went on. She turned. Stopped. Then bent over.

Glenda's round face came into full view. Her eyes grew round and her nostrils flared into twin circles. Then her mouth grew round. *A series of O's,* China

49

thought. If China hadn't been so scared, she would have laughed. China tilted her head and smiled. "Fancy meeting you here."

Glenda turned red and stood upright. Deedee and China crawled out from their hiding place and the three faced each other, not saying anything. Then Glenda's gaze moved toward the table. The open file folders were magnets, drawing her to them. As she looked, the red returned to her face. She turned a deeper and deeper red until China would have sworn she saw steam coming out of Glenda's ears.

"That's Lori's file. What are you doing with Lori's file?" Then she sputtered. "I know what you're doing with Lori's file. I knew you two were up to no good."

China felt like crawling back underneath the table. But Deedee stood with her hands on her hips. "The question is, what are *you* doing here? And how did you get in?"

Glenda stopped, the red flowing out of her face so fast she instantly became pale. Her mouth opened and closed like a gasping fish.

"China, I think we should report this."

A slow smile came across Glenda's face. "If you report me, then they'll know you were in here, too."

Now it was Deedee's turn to be a fish.

The three stood and regarded each other. Then Deedee closed the files and put them back into the open file drawer. She moved toward the door and motioned the other two to leave. She turned off the light and closed the door, making sure it was locked behind her. Glenda took the stairs two at a time and was out of the building before China and Deedee reached the door.

The next morning, China shoved the cardboard box holding all her clothes and belongings into its usual place under the bed while Deedee tied her massive red curls back with a yellow ribbon.

"Do you think Harrison is still alive?" China asked.

"I hope so."

The girls walked solemnly down the hall from the bedroom to the dining room. As usual, the rest of the Kiersey family had already finished their breakfast of eggs and toast. Bits of scrambled egg littered the table and floor. "What happened?" China asked. "Did a chicken explode here or what?"

Deedee's brothers and sisters howled with laughter.

"Girls," Mrs. Kiersey said, breezing in from the kitchen. "I hate to do this to you, but I've got to gather the kids and drive down the mountain. I need you to do the breakfast dishes."

"Mom," Deedee moaned. "This place is a disaster. We've got a day's worth of dishes waiting for us in the main camp kitchen."

"No big deal, Deeds," China said. "It'll be a new experience actually washing the dishes, rather than letting a machine eat them."

Mrs. Kiersey gathered the younger children and was gone.

With practiced speed, China scraped, stacked, and sorted the dishes on the dining table.

Mr. Kiersey rattled the newspaper, then closed it. "How is it going for you two girls over there?"

Deedee was on the floor, picking up egg and dropping it into a mug half-filled with cold coffee. "What could be worse than picking up egg off our dining room floor, Dad? Half the pieces are mushed into the cracks of the braided rug." She playfully punched at his foot until he moved it. She picked up another chunk of egg he had flattened. "With China there, working in the main kitchen isn't so bad."

"I heard you wanted the afternoon off to go riding. Is there some reason why this afternoon is so important?"

Deedee popped up so fast her head bonked on the underside of the table. "OW!" She crawled out, rubbing the crown of her head.

China put her stack of plates and silverware back on the table. "It just seemed like it would break up the week better," China said quickly. "Deedee said everyone on the staff got off one afternoon during the week."

"That's true, but I wondered if it had to be today. Someone named Glenda wanted this afternoon off too."

Sitting back on her heels, Deedee sighed. "It figures."

"But Rahja said you asked first. I told him I'd make sure it was important for you to have this afternoon off. Otherwise, I could let Glenda take the day off."

Deedee grabbed all the mugs and glasses off the table. "We planned to go riding because there were these other two campers going at the same time. We wanted to go with them."

China carried her stack into the kitchen, not wanting her face to give away the shock that Deedee had said something. But Deedee could do that somehow —state the truth in a way that didn't sound bad at all.

"Okay, then. I'll tell Rahja."

China turned on the water and started to rinse the plates. Deedee rummaged underneath the sink for the soap and dish drainer. "What's wrong with the riders, Dad? They all seem to have these bad attitudes."

"I've noticed they seem to live in their own world," Mr. Kiersey called from the dining room. "One quite different from ours. Most appear to be rather friendly, but a little on the strange side."

The noise of the water and dishes clattering together covered some of what Mr. Kiersey said. "Writers have always been known to be eccentric. Rather odd. They maintain plenty of secrecy. It must be the kind of work they do. Afraid someone will steal their precious stories."

"Don't their attitudes bother you?" China asked, as she plunged her hands into the sudsy water. Deedee took a cloth to wipe the crumbs and egg and spilled milk puddles off the table.

Mr. Kiersey folded his newspaper and laid it in a wooden box next to the fireplace. "Not really. I suppose

God made all of us different. You don't notice it so much when you get one of them alone. But when you get a bunch of them together, the "strange" factor is more obvious."

A pile of crumbs landed in Deedee's hand. "But Bill isn't like that."

Her father looked at her, confused. "The wrangler at the ranch? No, of course he's not."

The phone rang and Mr. Kiersey got up to answer it. "It's good for you girls to see how different people are."

China washed dishes while Deedee dried.

Mr. Kiersey hung up the phone. "Deedee, did you and China see anything suspicious around the Administration building last night?"

China kept her gaze on the sudsy water.

"Uh, no, Dad. Why?"

"Mr. Gibbons just called. Someone was in the file room last night. He said he saw you and China in the area around 9:00 and wondered if you saw anyone snooping around after he left."

"No, Dad, it was just me and China."

China felt her eyes grow wide. She forced herself to carefully rinse the silverware.

"Didn't the alarm go off?" Deedee asked.

"No. Someone who knew the alarm must have been in there and forgot to reset it. But Mr. Gibbons had checked on it about 8:00, and the alarm was set. Nothing seems to be missing or tampered with, so we hope everything's okay."

Mr. Kiersey pushed his fingertips together like spiders doing push-ups. "Well, if you hear anything at work today, let me know."

"Of course, Daddy."

China heard the front door close behind Mr. Kiersey. She scooped up a handful of bubbles and blew them at Deedee. "One of these days you're going to make me wet my pants."

Deedee just smiled.

Glenda abandoned her usual glare for simply treating the girls as though they were complete strangers needing directions on a street corner.

China and Deedee used their same system to wait tables. China was very disappointed that Belina and Marjean weren't sitting together. Walter kept his notebook open in his lap, occasionally writing things down during the meal.

China heard the usual snatches of conversation this group tended to say. "What kind of writing are you interested in?" was the most common question tossed about the table. Sometimes she heard the answer, sometimes she didn't. "Children" seemed to be a frequent answer. *Isn't it nice these people want to teach children how to ride. Maybe that's why there are so many women in the group. I wonder if I could teach children to ride someday.*

Most of the answers made more sense, like "action,"

"travel," and "adventure." She thought it odd that they categorized their riding, but she figured there really was a lot more to riding than Western and English styles. She didn't hear even one person mention English as the riding they were interested in. She did hear the word *Westerns* and assumed the guy who said that just didn't have his grammar quite right. But a couple of answers really threw her.

"What do you think 'poetry riding' is, Deedee?" China asked that afternoon, as they headed for their horse ride.

"Probably kind of like synchronized swimming. I saw a group of riders weaving in and out of each other in neat patterns in a parade once. My mom sighed and said it was like 'poetry in motion.'"

"What did you hear at lunch? Anything from Marjean?"

"No, just that she rides for a Chariot group of some sort."

"I didn't know you could ride for anyone, did you?" China pulled her tawny hair up and slipped a band around it to keep it off her neck. She wondered if the lemon juice she'd been combing into it was lightening the naturally dark roots. She'd always wished her hair was the same color on top as it was on bottom.

"I guess there's all sorts of riders' groups. Our wrangler, Bill, used to ride for the rodeo circuit. Then he rode for some other group I forgot the name of. A girl at school rides for some group that wants teenagers to have some good experiences in the outdoors."

China marched through the creek without taking off her ratty tennis shoes. "Ever heard of romance riding?"

Deedee shook her head, her thick curls swaying about her head. "No, I didn't. Do you think they dress up real pretty?"

"They've got those parades where the women wear gorgeous, ruffly dresses and stuff. Maybe that's it."

"One person said they rode for *Reader's Digest*. How do you ride for *Reader's Digest?*"

China's mind struggled to make sense of the information. Then she clapped her hands together. "I know! Maybe they have sponsors. You know, like Little League does, or some of the other team sports."

"I bet you're right. Maybe there's all kinds of competitions. It sure makes you realize how much you don't know about something, doesn't it?"

CHAPTER EIGHT

CHINA FELT LIKE A ROBOT as she moved through the wall of heat. Her arms swung at her sides in slow motion. Her legs felt like metal posts marching forward, and the sun baked the top of her head. She couldn't wait to get to the horses. She loved being on a horse in the heat. Just being up off the hot ground only a few feet was a lot cooler than walking.

Deedee wiped her damp forehead. "What's the plan?"

"We just get as close to Belina and Marjean as we can, and listen as much as we can. Maybe one of us should be ahead of them and one behind."

Deedee shook her head. "I don't think so. That would look too weird. Besides, they are professional riders. We'll look like idiots next to them."

Even if they hadn't known where they were going, they could smell the stables before they saw them. China and Deedee trudged up the slope, drinking in large gulps of the wonderful smell of horse.

Wrangler Bill was already astride his horse, as was everyone else going on the trail ride. With relief, China noticed Marjean and Belina were in the rear of the line.

"Are you the last two riders?" Bill asked. "If I'd known it was you two, I would have left you behind. You're two minutes late."

Deedee smiled. "You'll forgive me, Bill. You always do."

Bill snorted a horsey sound.

China swung up on a buckskin oddly named Silver. At once she was giddily happy. The whole horse thing filled her with incredible feelings. Horseflesh—warm, dusty, full of flies. Twitching tails. Snorts, low rumblings. Stomping feet. China adored horses when she was around them, but she didn't live and breathe them in her off hours.

The dry trail blew up small clouds of dust as hooves pounded it. A slight clatter sounded when hooves connected with stones instead. The scenery during the first few minutes was green and lush. Thick trees, cooler air. Pure forest. Then it opened up to a new beauty . . . panoramic scenery.

"This is incredible," Belina said, her head constantly swiveling back and forth in order to catch all the sights without missing anything. She held onto the saddle horn with a white-knuckled grip, even as her horse walked. She slid all over the saddle, unable to stay in one place.

"Makes you wish you were a cowgirl," Marjean said. "Riding the open range." She, too, clasped her saddle horn with a death grip. Her backside filled the saddle, but she still managed to slide around like Belina.

"These greenhorns are *riders?*" Deedee said to China.

China snorted. "Even I ride better than they do."

Belina and Marjean's running conversation on how beautiful everything was began to bore Deedee and China. Eventually they blocked out the two women's inane commentary and talked between themselves.

"We've got to make time to see Magda," China told Deedee. "I miss her like crazy."

"And Bologna," Deedee added.

"And Bologna." China looked around, then started to laugh. "Notice anything different?"

Deedee's brows pulled together. She looked up the ravine and over the chaparral to the canyon beyond. "No."

"Walter's not here."

Deedee gasped. "Are you sure? I wonder if he's okay. Maybe we should go looking for him."

Both girls laughed.

"I've gotten used to seeing him sneak around so much, I kind of miss him."

Deedee nodded. "I guess I started to block it out. I didn't even notice him after a while."

Suddenly China was aware that Marjean was saying something significant as she pointed up the ravine and said, "There would be a good place."

Belina shook her head. "The sound would echo."

"No, just to put the body."

Belina shook her head again. "Too obvious. We've got to think of something better than that."

China hit herself in the arm. *I should have been listening!*

Deedee nodded, knowing what China would have said if she'd spoken aloud.

Marjean chuckled. "Remember what started all this? Burying Grandpa in the backyard. That brought us closer than anything."

Belina put her head back and laughed a high-pitched, Hee, hee, hee. "I never thought I'd do that. But it came out great. We really should work together more often."

"It's a lot more fun, and it takes less time to complete the whole job. Two people brainstorming this are better than one."

"They are totally SICK," Deedee mouthed to China. *"Burying a grandfather in their backyard and laughing about it?"* China put her finger to her lips.

The girls rode quietly behind the two women, watching every move the writers made. Everywhere the women looked, the girls looked too. Every comment they made, the girls made careful mental notes.

"You know, Marjean, there must be a cave somewhere."

"An abandoned mine! That's it! Those things have holes with no bottom. They'd never find him there."

"But should I get him there dead or alive?" Belina asked.

"I don't know. You could make it look like an accident."

"Why would it have to be an accident? Everyone in the cult wants him dead. No one else would miss him."

Marjean nodded her head and seemed lost in thought.

"To make things more interesting, maybe I should introduce someone who would care that he's gone. Someone who would notice."

Marjean smiled. "Very good idea. It should be a woman." Then she frowned and shook her head. "I'd still like to see him escape alive."

"They'd track him down and find him. There are too many of them. And how would he assimilate into society? A man with no past. No work record. A man who wouldn't really know how to behave in society once he got there."

China swallowed hard and threw a look at Deedee. Deedee didn't catch it. She was too engrossed in the scene playing out before her.

"I've never killed anyone before," Belina said finally. "I'm not real sure how to go about it."

"I'm just surprised a Christian is telling you to do it."

China felt her jaw drop. Deedee lurched, almost falling off her horse.

"Me too. But I guess murder happens everywhere, not just in the secular market."

China couldn't control herself. *"Market?"* she mouthed to Deedee.

Belina sighed. "I guess it does make the thing more realistic." She sighed again, looking off toward the mountain peak. "What am I going to do? I only have a couple more days."

Marjean's face lit up. "I know. There's a book out about deadly weapons or poisons or something. It's for people who write mysteries."

"But that's not us," Belina moaned.

"Maybe there will be something in it to help us. I'll go to the library when we're done with the ride. You go to your room and brainstorm some more. It'll come to you. It always does."

China sneezed. "Uh, excuse me," she said lamely.

Marjean and Belina turned around, looking surprised that the girls were there. "Oh!" Marjean said. "It's you two."

China gulped.

Marjean turned to Belina. "Our waitresses."

A light of recognition shone in Belina's eyes. "That's right." Then her face grew dark. "You won't tell anyone what we've been saying, will you? I mean, no one at the conference?"

The girls just looked at her, not knowing what to do or how to react.

Marjean spoke up. "I know you don't understand.

But it really is *very* important that you don't tell any-one. It could ruin things."

Belina nodded. "This is a very sticky business. People steal ideas all the time."

"Not meaning to, of course," Marjean added. "It's just that with such fertile imaginations, you never know when someone is accidentally going to ruin what you've got going. We like to keep things real quiet until it's all over and done with."

"Then it doesn't matter what people do with the information," Belina said.

Marjean turned back again to look at the girls. Her eyes narrowed. "You won't say anything, will you? It wouldn't be fair to Belina at all."

China blurted out, "What about Harrison? Isn't this all being unfair to Harrison?"

Belina's eyes widened at the mention of Harrison. "I didn't recall saying his name . . ."

Marjean cut in. "In this business some things can't be helped. Things have to be realistic. Besides, if you don't do it yourself, someone else does."

"And when they do," Belina grumbled, "they usually botch it up and make a mess out of all your hard work. It's not worth it."

Marjean shrugged. "So you do what they tell you to do. If you want to keep your contract and get future offers, you have to do it with a smile, whether you like it or not."

Deedee looked numb. Or like her mind had just left

on an around-the-world vacation without her.

China shook her head. "I don't think I'd like to work for people like that."

"When God gives you a gift, you use it the best way you can, even if it isn't your first choice," Marjean said in her throaty voice.

China couldn't think of a reply to that. Her mind wouldn't even spit out something that remotely made sense. Just individual words popped into her head. Words that made no sense when linked together. *Gift. Kill. God gives. Use?*

Within moments, Belina had found the perfect spot to unload the body. Around a bend there was a trail wide enough to take a horse dragging a travois up a ravine. At the end, they figured there was an old mine. The cuttings in the rock wall gave indication that it was a manmade ravine, not a natural one, although nature had obviously made good use of it.

China and Deedee took special note of the place so they could return later. *At least we can show the police where he ends up,* China thought sadly.

Back at the corral, the girls absently unsaddled their horses. The other riders had disappeared quickly after dismounting. Belina and Marjean smiled at the girls and thanked them for promising to be quiet.

"I didn't promise anything," China grumbled. "I can't believe these two."

"I can't believe they are getting these orders from a Christian," Deedee said.

"I'm so confused," China confessed. "I think we're just going to have to keep watching and waiting."

Deedee sighed. "I only hope we can figure all this out before Harrison dies." She shook her head. "They are such nice people, really."

"Deedee! How can you say that?"

"They are. I wish they weren't planning a murder, because I think I'd like them a lot."

"I think we should tell your dad," China said.

"What? YOU want to tell my dad?"

"Well, kinda, sorta. I mean we should start out beating around the bush. You do that real well, so I think you should do it."

"When?"

"Right now. Call him. Doesn't the stable have a phone?"

Deedee hoisted the saddle onto the rack. "Yeah."

Outside the corral, Bill stripped horses of their saddles. Deedee got permission to use the phone. As the girls disappeared into the dark stable, Bill called to them. "You have to bang the receiver before you can hear very well. There's a lot of static on the line. Too much dirt around here. Gets into everything."

Deedee dialed her dad's extension, and he answered right away. "Dad, I've got to tell you something very important." She paused a moment then yelled. "DAD, I'VE GOT TO TELL YOU SOMETHING VERY IMPORTANT." She paused another moment, then hit the phone on the table, which already bore dents from other receiver whackings. "Dad, these riders are terrible. I don't think they are who they say they are. I think they're phonies."

China stuck her ear next to Deedee's. The connection was so bad she could barely make out Mr. Kiersey's answers. "They're phones?" he asked.

"NO. PHONIES. FAKES. They can't ride well at all."

"I'm not surprised. There's a lot of beginners in the group. I don't think this is something you girls should worry about."

"Dad, they're planning a MURDER."

"I guess that's part of their job. I've been hearing a lot about what's required of them. I don't think I'd like that job either. Too much pressure."

Deedee sagged next to China. Instead of talking, a little sound huffed out of her. "Huh, huh, huh," the little noise came.

"Listen Deedee. I've got to run. We've got some staffing problems I've got to take care of right now. Don't let them bother you. I told you writers are a little strange and they live in a different world. If what they talk about bothers you, just leave them alone."

Deedee stood with the phone stuck to her ear. She stared at the holes in the stable wall, bright stars of light in the dark wood. China tried to take the receiver out of her hand. Deedee clung to it, still staring. China tugged on the phone. "Deedee, let go! Come on. We need to go to work." Deedee remained lifeless. Catatonic. "DEEDS!" China shouted. She rapped her knuckles on top of Deedee's head. "Hey. Wake up!" She knocked Deedee's head one more time, and Deedee came back to life. She sank down in the metal folding chair, dropping the phone.

"I can't believe it. Even my dad has gone nuts. This whole world is crazy."

China picked up the receiver and replaced it in the cradle. "I think we're just dreaming all this. Our imaginations just got away with us. We're kind of like Dorothy in *Wizard of Oz*. We'll wake up and Belina and Marjean will be, uh, like our stuffed animals or something."

"Pinch me," Deedee said.

China took a hunk of arm flesh and squeezed lightly.

"No, harder."

China took a tiny piece and squeezed as hard as she could.

"OW!" Deedee yanked her arm away.

"I just did what you told me to."

"We're not asleep, China. This whole thing is real. We're living a nightmare where all the things that used to be bad are now okay. Even my dad is caught up in it."

"Maybe they've drugged him," China offered. "I've heard of people doing that."

They stepped out of the dark into bright, hot sunlight. China looked at her watch and moaned. "Deeds. It's 3:30. We missed B.T.'s phone call."

"Or Mr. Gleckenspiel." Deedee walked away slowly.

"Not that I care at this moment. Not that I will ever care again."

"And we're going to be late for work if we don't hurry."

"Does it really matter? Nothing matters any more."

CHAPTER NINE

CHINA DIDN'T LIKE BEING LEFT alone with her thoughts as they walked toward the main camp. She didn't like it when her brain had too much information. It was like starting a two thousand-piece jigsaw puzzle after having gotten the edges together. None of the rest of the parts fit. Everything lay there in mumbo-jumbo, making no sense. Hours could go by and the pieces still didn't fit. Eventually she figured she had the wrong pieces. Then her mind kept sorting through the scattered thoughts, trying to find something that fit with something else. But nothing did. *Two women were planning a murder, and no one seemed to care.*

She and Deedee walked side by side, each involved in their own disturbing thoughts. Ahead, a group of high school campers laughed and shoved each other toward the creek. The one who landed in the water started heaving water with his massive hands. A couple of others chose large rocks to use as a discus. Like ballerinas with a balance problem, they spun around and let the rocks fly. Deedee marched forward, not paying much attention to it all.

"Thompson! You fool! I'll cream you, I swear!" called the soaked guy in the water.

"Just try, Harrison, just try."

A punky kid standing off to the side covered his face when two of the bigger guys approached him. "Lay off, Gordon. This isn't fair. Pick on someone your own size."

"It's more fun watching you squirm."

The girls sized up the scene, trying to decide how to go around them without getting caught in the melee.

The punky kid, dodging the two guys playing with him, suddenly stopped. "Hey, guys. Harrison. Quit it with the water. Let the ladies go by." He gave a sweeping bow that would have been incredibly attractive on a taller, smoother guy. On him, it looked silly.

"Thank you," Deedee said, her voice dull.

Halfway into the group, China looked at the guy in the water and put out her hand to stop Deedee. "Harrison," she said softly.

Deedee looked at her. "What are you talking about?"

"Harrison. They called him Harrison."

Deedee's whole body tensed. She looked at the guy standing in the water. She leaned toward China. "Don't you think he's a little young?"

"They didn't say how old Harrison was."

"Yeah, but they were talking about marrying him."

China snorted. "They don't have any other . . . what's the word? . . . any conscience about anything else, why would they care whether Harrison is seventeen or seventy?"

Deedee walked up to the edge of the creek and called to Harrison. "Can we talk to you for a minute?"

"Oooo! Harrison," chorused the testosterone-driven group behind them.

The male bonding society gathered around the girls. Deedee looked up at them, most towering over her. "Alone."

"Oooo-hooo!" came the newest chorus.

Harrison trudged out of the water. "Listen," China told him. "We have good reason to believe your life is in danger."

Harrison cocked his head to look at the girls, each one in turn. Then he looked up at the guys behind them and whirled his finger around his ear.

"I know it sounds crazy," China said, "but you've got to listen to us. Someone is going to try to kill you before Friday."

The guys had moved in again. "Cool," one said.

"His mom did say he'd be lucky to live to see his eighteenth birthday," Thompson said, nodding his head.

Harrison took on a look of fake fear. "Mom's here? Hide me. What'll I do?"

"There are these two women," Deedee said. "We think you might know Belina."

"Never heard of her," Harrison said. He looked at his friends. They all shook their heads.

"She's been hanging with this woman named Marjean and they've been talking about how they have to kill Harrison because he knows too much."

Every one of the guys burst into major laughter . . . all except Harrison. "Harrison knows too much? Harrison don't know nothin'," piped up one of the boys.

"He knows how to find the cutest babes," another guy interjected.

Everyone nodded their agreement.

"I know a lot," Harrison protested.

China looked up at Harrison, her face begging him to believe her. "The group is upset because you know all about what they're doing, and now that you're trying to leave, they want you dead."

Harrison paled. "Are you sure? The group knows I'm trying to leave?"

China and Deedee nodded.

Thompson slugged his friend in the shoulder. "What group, man? You copping out on us? You got something going you haven't told us about?"

Harrison shook his head. Not like he was saying no. But like he was trying to throw an unwanted thought out of it. His face lost the look of pale fear and he became a crazy kid again. "Nah." To China and Deedee, he said, "Hey. Thanks for the warning. I'll be cool. Don't worry. Besides, who can knock me off with these goons hanging around all the time?"

The guys all laughed, then took the macho stance —crossed arms and spread legs.

"How're they gonna do it?" Harrison asked.

"We don't know," Deedee said. "They haven't decided yet."

"But we do know where they're going to throw your body," China said.

"Down a mine shaft," Deedee said.

"Cool," Thompson said. "Show us so we can go visit. Send flowers. Throw Joey in after." Everyone laughed except the punky kid.

"Not funny, Thompson," Joey said in his squeaky voice.

"Thanks for the info," Harrison told them. "We gotta go get chocolate chip shakes now."

As they parted ways, China saw Harrison making the crazy sign around his ear again. Thompson said a little too loudly, "There's crazy people everywhere, man. Mike Harrison, you always seem to collect more than your share."

Deedee let her hair loose. "They don't believe us. No one believes us."

"Should we tell Magda?"

"We should stay away from Magda. She reads you like a book, China. You take one step near her and she's going to know something's wrong."

"But she'd believe me. She might be able to help us."

"What could she do? Nothing. I think we should keep this between us. If my own dad won't do anything about it, the cops won't. No one will believe us."

Back at the main camp, conferees were every-where. Kids covered the place, screaming and run-ning helter-skelter. Blue notebooks with horses on the cover lay open on laps, and the writers were busy reading and writing in them.

"This is the strangest riders' conference," Deedee muttered." No one hardly looks at a horse."

Across the street, Walter was hitching along, mum-bling happily to himself. When he saw the girls, a laugh popped out of his mouth sounding like a hiccup.

"Whatever secret he's got, he's sure delighted with himself," Deedee said.

"Look," China said quietly, nudging Deedee and nodding toward a group of trees. Beneath them, Belina and Marjean sat on a rock wall. They kept pointing at a notebook, talking, gesturing, shaking their heads, and writing. Belina sat up, let out a grunt of frustra-tion, ripped out the page, crumpled it and threw it in the garbage can. She rifled through a few more pages, ripped them out of the notebook and threw them away also.

"I've had it!" she said to Marjean. "I'm going to my room." With that, she slammed her notebook shut, stood up, and walked away. Marjean looked after her, sighed, then closed her own notebook, and followed Belina.

"Perfect," China said. She looked around and quickly covered the ground between her and the garbage can with silent steps. Deedee followed her. China leaned over, dug around a little, and came out with several wadded up pieces of paper. She held them up like a hard-earned trophy.

Deedee smiled at her. "Oh, China. You do think!" Then her face changed from excitement to surprise.

"STOP!" growled a voice behind China. "What do you think you're doing?"

China slowly turned. Sour, hot breath reeking of old coffee, old tortilla chips, and old age poured out of Walter's angry mouth. The wrinkles in his face were etched furrows ready for spring planting. His eyes narrowed, the pupils little pinpoints of black in cloudy blue irises. "How dare you. How DARE you! Those papers are none of your business. You little thieves. You steal from others. I know the likes of you. You stole from me and sold it all to Hollywood. Well, I'm not going to let you steal another. Even if it's not mine. They say it don't happen. But here's proof. I thought I'd come to a Christian place, hoping there'd be Christian people doing Christian things. But no. It's the same everywhere. It don't matter if you're a Christian or a heathen. Everywhere you go people steal. It's all for money. Money is the root of it all . . ."

China pulled herself out of the trance that held her tied to that awful breath. "Come on, Deedee. Let's get out of here."

"Wait!" Walter said, breaking his endless tirade.

"Give me those papers first. They don't belong to you." He grabbed China's wrists and held fast. "I bet you've stolen mine, too. I bet you take them and tell your producer friend all about me."

China squirmed. "No way. They were in the trash. You don't know who they belong to."

"Belina. You can't have her ideas."

"Is the whole world on Belina's side?" Deedee asked, incredulous.

China clamped her jaws shut and concentrated on her wrists. She tightened them, closed her eyes, and bent her knees. Elbows down, she put all her weight low, beneath her wrists. All at once she stood quickly, breaking free from Walter's grasp. "Come on!" she said to Deedee as she ran, stuffing the wads of paper inside her shirt.

"Woohoo!" shouted Harrison's group. "Yeah, Baby!"

China didn't care. She just ran toward the kitchen, hoping Deedee was behind her. Steam boiled out the back door, a never-ending plume of smoke. Deedee came to a screeching halt behind China. "It looks like when God was a pillar of cloud."

"Maybe we should ask the pillar what's going on around here." China looked beyond Deedee to see if Walter had followed. She figured if he could run, he couldn't run very fast.

Deedee pulled open the screen door, letting even more steam roil out the door. They were immediately enveloped into the cloud. Deedee batted the steam.

"Whew! Out of the hot day and into the cooking pot," she said.

"I don't think that's how it goes," China said. "Do you think Walter's got Alzheimer's or something?"

"Probably. He sure doesn't make sense very often."

"At least he's not one of the bad guys."

"Like Belina and Marjean?"

China nodded.

"You know, I always thought of people who did stuff like this as kind of smarmy looking. Greasy hair, dirty clothes, three days of not shaving."

"I didn't get a good look at their legs," China said. "Maybe they haven't shaved."

Deedee rolled her eyes. "China!" She whacked her arm.

"I know what you mean. I always think of bad guys as grungy men wearing black hats, spitting tobacco, and looking like they hadn't bathed in years."

"You've been watching too many Westerns."

"What's a girl supposed to do when the only missionary with a VCR has stacks of Westerns?"

Glenda appeared from inside the stainless steel maze. "I'm glad you guys are back. Kyle is sick now. We need to hustle to get dinner ready." Her whole body oozed with fake niceness.

"What's with the honey-dripping smile?" Deedee hissed into China's ear.

"I think it's an oil slick. It just looks like honey, but it would destroy the water supply."

Deedee swallowed a bubble of laughter.

"What do you guys want to do? Fill food bins for the Tribal Villages? Or help Rahja with the spare ribs?"

"We get a choice?" China asked, incredulous.

Deedee elbowed her in the ribs. "We'll fill food bins for the Tribal Villages." She returned the fake smile.

Glenda started to stare at China's chest. China looked down at the lumpy part that should be smooth. She smiled at Glenda and said with a straight face. "Oops. They slipped."

Deedee choked. Together they headed for the stairs to the pit.

CHAPTER TEN

"**I** THOUGHT WE COULD TALK better down here," Deedee said, as they clumped down the stairs. "The trucks back up to the loading dock and pick up food for the villages," she explained. "So the food prep is done down here, too."

She opened the dumbwaiter. "Nothing in here yet. Let's get the sandwich stuff and milk ready first."

China ignored her. She plopped herself in a dry corner behind Huge Harold. Reaching inside her shirt, she removed the wads of paper.

The heading on the first paper read, HARRISON'S MURDER in neatly printed block letters. The rest of the paper was a mess. Some handwritten, some printed, lots crossed out.

Gun . . . too easy—they have no guns anyway.
Push over falls . . . too messy . . . body to dispose of.
Car accident . . . he doesn't drive.
Hanging . . . he's too strong. He wouldn't allow it.

80

Knife . . . too messy. How would cult explain the blood?

Blunt object . . . I couldn't bear it.

How do we get him to the old mine . . . dead or alive? Tell him one of the kids is missing and get him to go with a search party?

There were other things written, but China couldn't make them out.

"China, we have to get to work," Deedee said, looking over her shoulder.

She sighed deeply. "I think we've done all we can."

"How can you give up?"

"I think I gave up when I found out my own dad doesn't even care."

Deedee put out her hand and helped China to her feet. China folded the crumpled papers and put them in her pocket.

The fast work helped them take their minds off Harrison, but only a little bit. The dumbwaiter brought them buckets of food to distribute in several plastic bins that went to each tribe in the Tribal Villages. Tonight one bin had chicken legs, one had corn on the cob, one had mashed potatoes, and one had gravy. Each tribe also got a loaf of bread and a butter tub filled with jelly and one with peanut butter. Small cartons of milk had to be counted out, thirty for each tribe.

"Why do you think Glenda hates us?" Deedee asked.

"I have a better question," China said. "Why was she in the file room?"

"Maybe the two go together." Deedee tried to lift a case of milk onto the top of the stack.

"Here," China said, "let me do that." She hoisted it up with ease.

Deedee shook her head. "How do you do that?"

"So why was Glenda in the file room?"

"She said something about one of the files on the table. That we'd done enough damage."

"Does she know about Harrison? Seems like everyone else does."

Deedee shook her head slowly. "She seemed to hate us before we even saw Belina and Marjean."

"Not before we saw them," China reminded her. "But for sure before we talked to them."

They counted more milk and China swung more crates into stacks of four. Deedee stood up. "I know! Maybe she's a big fan of B.T.'s and heard we're friends with him."

China nodded. "Or this Lori she talks about wants to be his girlfriend. And she thinks we're taking the place of Lori as B.T.'s girlfriend."

After the milk was done, they started the sticky task of scooping jelly out of huge tin cans and putting it in butter tubs. "Maybe she wants to work at Eelapuash," China suggested. "It's a lot more fun over there than it is here. Maybe she's mad at me because I work over there."

A head popped into the small work room. "How are you guys doing?" Glenda asked.

Deedee blushed.

"Fine," China said. "Just fine."

"I've brought someone who wants to talk with you guys."

"First," China said. "I've noticed that you aren't too thrilled with us. And I kind of wondered why. I thought maybe you wanted to work at Eelapuash. Is that something you've wanted to do?"

Glenda's eyes narrowed to their catlike slits. "What? Now you want my job, too? One thing isn't enough for you? Are you trying to push me out like you did Lori? Not on your life." She spun around and left the room.

As soon as she left, Marjean and Belina appeared at the door. China tried to smile. Deedee made a big deal over scooping balls of peanut butter into plastic tubs. She put the lids carefully on the tubs, snapping them shut.

"I don't know if I should believe a tired old man or not," Belina started. She looked furious. Her eyes flashed. Her small hands clenched into fists and released again.

Marjean butted in. "I thought you promised to stay out of this."

"We didn't really promise," China said, trying to sound like she was strong. She hoped they couldn't tell her knees were shaking.

"Look," Belina said. "I've worked long and hard on

this. And I don't want two kids spoiling it for me. I don't think it's that big of a deal for you to keep out."

She stared at China until China looked away.

"Give me the papers." Belina put her hand out.

China didn't look up. She held still.

"Give me the papers," Belina repeated.

"No," China said in a soft voice.

"What?" Belina asked, incredulous.

Instead of answering, China bolted from the room. She ran to the dumbwaiter and climbed in, sitting cross-legged. She leaned out and punched the button to close the doors and send the elevator up to the kitchen. The tiny elevator lurched and groaned with its added weight. China closed her eyes against the putrid darkness. The rotting smells of spilled food wafted up from the shaft. She took shallow breaths to minimize the amount of spoiled air she took in.

It seemed like forever before the little box shivered to a stop. The door opened to the angry faces of Belina, Marjean, and Glenda. Just as Glenda shouted, "What in the worl . . ." a slender hand shot out and punched the button to send her down again.

Back in the pit, China unfolded herself and climbed out to the waiting anger of the three women.

"This is NOT a toy, China," Glenda scolded.

"I want my papers back," Belina demanded.

"Rahja's going to hear about this," Glenda said, sounding happy she had something to report. To Marjean and Belina she said, "I'll talk to you later."

She turned on her heel and marched upstairs.

"I want my papers," Belina said, sounding like a pouting child.

"Forget it, Belina," Marjean said, exhaustion in her voice. "There's nothing in the papers anyway."

"It's the principle of the thing."

"They're only kids, Belina."

"But Walter said they were talking to the authorities. We can't let that happen."

"First of all," Marjean reasoned, "would the authorities listen to a couple of kids?"

Belina sized up China and Deedee. A look of foolishness covered her face.

"Second," Marjean continued, "since when did Walter ever make sense? He's always paranoid about something."

Belina nodded. "You're right. It's just that if any of this got out, we'd be dead. Finished. Ruined."

Marjean put her arm around Belina. "You're under too much stress. Now you're over-reacting. A couple of kids can't ruin your plans."

They walked out, an odd couple. Tall, big-boned Marjean with her arm around tiny Belina.

"Now do I feel stupid," China said. "Talk about over-reacting." She leaned back against the wall and let it support her as she slid down to the floor.

"Don't," Deedee said, a silly grin taking over her face. "Now we've got proof that a murder is being planned."

"No we don't," China moaned. "I stuffed the papers through a hole in the dumbwaiter. I thought Belina was going to beat me to the top. And I thought we could retrieve them later. But we can't. The whole thing is sealed up."

"Great! Just great."

Just then three burly workers walked in. "Food ready for the Villages?"

"Almost," Deedee said. She walked to the small prep room. "You guys can start with the main dinner bins. We'll be done with the peanut butter in a minute."

CHAPTER ELEVEN

SERVING DINNER THAT EVENING was miserable for China and Deedee. With four people glaring at them, and their own inner turmoil, it was all they could do to smile and be friendly. After dinner, they eagerly went to the pit and helped Nigel with the dishes until he was called to help upstairs.

"After a day like this, I need a shower," China said, when Nigel had gone.

Deedee shrugged.

"I need a shower!" China whined, as if she were a child crying out for chocolate. "I need a shower and I need it NOW."

Deedee took on her role of pacifying mother. "Okay, dear. We'll get you a shower as soon as we get back home."

China marched up to Huge Harold and flipped the hot water switch to the off position. Then she flung herself onto the plastic prongs. "Goodbye, cruel world!" she called, as the conveyor belt propelled her slowly toward Harold's stomach.

"China!" Deedee shrieked. "You've lost your mind! Get off there."

"No, no," China said in a melodramatic voice. "There is no other choice for one such as me. I shall discover what it was like to be Jonah."

With that, she was swallowed. Huge Harold's many rubber-dangling tongues swished over her. "It tickles!" China cried out in overwhelming giggles. The giggles turned to water-logged guffaws, and then coughing and sputtering.

Deedee knocked on Harold's metal sides."You okay in there? China?"

In response, she only got an underwater shriek of laughter.

Momentarily, China's head reappeared out the other end of Harold's stomach. More rubber dangly tongues swished, absorbing some of the water pouring off China.

"This is so cool," China sputtered. "You really ought to try it, Deedee."

"You did such a great job, I think I'll pass."

Deedee turned off the conveyor, and China rolled over on her back and just lay there dripping. "I don't dry as fast as the dishes, do I?"

Deedee looked at her watch. "Let's get out of here. If we move fast enough, we can see Rick and Magda on the way home."

China rolled over. "It's not on the way home. We have to pass your home to go see them."

"A mere technicality, my dear. You want to go or not?"

"Just giving you a bad time."

They left through the door that led to the loading dock and went down the stairs into the deepening dusk.

They linked arms and skipped, singing the *Wizard of Oz* song as they went. In the middle of the Battlefield, they flopped on their backs to watch the emerging stars.

"Can you count them?" Deedee asked China. "I love to count stars. When I think God has forgotten me, I count stars."

China lay with her head on her arms, looking into the vast bowl of sky. "How can you count the stars? There's so many."

"That's why I love to count them. If God cares about the names of all these round pieces of rock, I bet He really cares about me."

China was silent for a long time. Then softly she said, "I knew God really cared about me when he let me stay the summer. This has been the absolute best . . ."

"Twenty-five, twenty-six," Deedee counted stars under her breath.

"But does God care about Harrison?"

Deedee stopped counting and flipped over onto her side to face China. "We forgot to even tell God about Harrison."

"But the whole thing is so impossible," China said.

"There's a verse that says something like 'with man it's impossible, but nothing is impossible for God.' I think it's in Luke."

"How do you know all these verses?" China asked.

"Some camp speakers harp on the same topic over and over. It gets pounded into your head whether you like it or not."

"God?" China said, searching the sky for something that would look like God. "You know all about this Harrison thing. Can you please help him not to be killed?"

"And help Belina, Marjean, and the other people telling them to do this to be caught," Deedee added.

China sat up and brushed off her hands. "Time to go see Magda and Rick."

Deedee groaned as she sat up.

Suddenly a shot rang out.

"What was that?"

"You tell me, Deedee. You live here."

They heard another shot. Then one more.

"Let's get out of here," Deedee said. They jumped up and took off for home.

When they burst into the Kiersey home, startling Mrs. Kiersey, Deedee blurted out what they'd heard.

"Deedee, there's nothing to worry about. We hear shots like that on occasion. Sometimes it's people doing target practice. Sometimes it's hunters."

"At night?"

"I agree that's a little odd, but we've had stranger

things happen. And there has always been a logical explanation."

Mrs. Kiersey leaned forward to get a button off the lamp stand. "Oh. There was a strange phone call for you girls today." She picked up a piece of paper lying next to the button. "A Mr. Simon Carnegie from *Star World Enterprise* tabloid called." She looked up from the paper. "Isn't that one of those trashy newspapers at the grocery check out stand?"

"It's another of B.T.'s silly jokes, Mom," Deedee said, a smile taking over her face.

"Well, he wants you to call—no matter how late."

Deedee went to the phone. She yelled to China when the call went through and China picked up the extension phone in the living room.

"MISTER Carnegie!" Deedee said, with all the absurd tone she could muster. "What a *pleasant* and *charming* surprise!"

China pinched her nose. "We would be so pleezed to give you any information on Mister Brian Thomas that you wish to have."

"But!" Deedee said. "We can only give interviews in person . . ."

"And only at a price!" China added. "Tomorrow night, 8:30 P.M."

"I'll be there," came the sleazy reply.

The girls hung up the phone, collapsing into a heap of giggles.

The laughter didn't last long. Once in bed, the heavy

weight that lay on their chests returned.

The next morning after the rest of the family had breakfast, China and Deedee got up. A sober Mr. Kiersey quickly hung up the phone.

"What's wrong, Daddy?"

"A high school kid is missing. Say a prayer."

The girls grabbed a half-empty box of Lucky Charms and took off for their hideout. They didn't say a word until they got inside.

"Should we go to the mine and see if we can find him?" Deedee asked.

China chewed on her cheek, then grabbed a handful of cereal. She picked out all the yellow moons and tossed them back into the box. She wanted so much to say something, but nothing came to her mind. Eating seemed the only thing to do with her mouth at the moment. Not that she was hungry. But it did give her something to do.

"I don't believe it!" Deedee hissed. "Look who's coming!"

From one direction came Marjean, and the from the other came Belina.

"Did you have a nice morning walk?" Belina asked, her voice high-pitched with excitement.

"Very nice. Why are *you* so jazzed?"

"I did it! I did it! And you're going to love how I did it. I'm so happy." Belina spun around and around. She looked like a kid who had just been told she gets to go to Disneyland for her birthday.

"Yeah? And? Did you let them know?"

"Of course. I called them immediately. They were thrilled with what I did. They said they're ready to sign me up for another since I did such a good job and did it so promptly. They said that's what they like. So they'll be looking at my next one as soon as I can get it to them."

"Great, Belina! I'm so jealous! But you're incredibly gifted. I don't know if I could ever do what you do."

"Don't be jealous, Marjean. You're incredible with kids. I could never do that. We're just gifted in different areas, that's all. Come on. Let's go celebrate."

China felt her whole body droop.

"I can't believe it's too late," Deedee said. "I can't believe it."

They didn't say another word as tears dripped silently down their cheeks. They sat so still, the spiders began to spin their webs once more.

At work, Glenda pushed the girls into a corner. "Did you hear? They found a body."

"What?" "When?" The girls asked together.

"Just about an hour ago. Near the horse trail. Gruesome, huh?" Glenda shivered.

"Who?"

"The rangers."

"No, I mean, who was it?" China asked. Her heart pounded. *As if we didn't know.*

"They don't know."

I know. Deedee knows.

Glenda's voice got dramatic and she moved her arms about in large gestures. "Some guy with 'no past, no family, no records.' Cool, huh?"

"A guy is murdered and you say, 'cool'?" Deedee asked, incredulous.

Glenda's face clouded. "Who said he was murdered?"

"We heard gunshots last night," Deedee said.

"I don't think he was shot."

"Well, people don't just *die*, do they?" China asked pointedly.

"Sometimes they do," Glenda said. "They think this guy did. He was skinny and stuff. Was probably hungry."

"I think I know who did it," Deedee said.

"No one 'did it', Deedee. He just died. That's all."

"How can you be so sure?"

The two girls stared at each other.

Just then the swinging door to the dining room swung open and Belina swept in, Marjean at her heels. "Glenda! It's done! I thought you should be one of the first to know. Thanks for your prayers."

They prayed about this? China wondered.

"You're welcome." Glenda smiled the first genuine smile the girls had seen. "I'm so glad."

"We need to get to class. Talk to you later."

"Congratulations," Glenda called after Belina, who

waved in response, the swinging door cutting off their view of her.

China looked carefully at Glenda. "Where do you know them from?"

"Oh, I've known them from way back. We used to . . ." Her eyes grew dark. "It's really none of your business. You guys better get to work. There's a lot of cornbread to make before lunch."

CHAPTER TWELVE

"**W**E'VE GOT TO DO SOMETHING," China said over bowls full of cornbread batter.

"Like what?" Deedee looked around to see if anyone was listening. "You're the one with the imaginative brain. *You* think of something."

"Okay, okay. Let me think."

China's brain spun out of control. At times like this it seemed her brain was a living thing separate from the rest of her, and she was just going along for the ride. Right now she worked and did what Deedee told her to, but she really didn't pay any attention. Her thoughts were like debris picked up and whirled madly inside a tornado that sped by too fast for her to grasp onto any one thing. She'd learned long ago to let the process take care of itself. Not to force it. Not to try to understand it. She could make a judgment call after she saw what answers her brain came up with.

No answer came before lunch. During lunch the

tables of "riders" were alive with zaniness. One came dressed in a wild outfit claiming to be "the motivator." She had on a man's shoes that flopped like clown shoes on her small feet, a wig that stuck out in all directions, glasses, and a plastic water rifle tucked under her arm. She put on a skit and the "riders" were in hysterics. Belina laughed the most.

Her happiness dug into China like a thorn in a lion's paw. Not enough to cause damage, but enough to cause great aggravation and anger. By the end of lunch, China had a plan.

"Nigel," China said sweetly, while leaning up against Huge Harold. "If we do an absolutely terrific job, can we leave early? You know, don't tell anyone." She smiled the most endearing smile she could conjure up.

Nigel looked at her, his mouth moving as if he chewed a great wad of gum. "I don't know. I don't believe that is honest. And I must insist on honesty in all things."

Deedee wagged her head. "We don't want to get paid for the time we're not here or anything. You can dock us that pay. We just have something incredibly urgent that must be taken care of this afternoon."

Nigel looked at his watch, then looked around the room. "If you can get every single thing done that needs to be done, I will let you go. But you must never ask again."

Both girls shook their heads quickly. "We won't ask again."

"Honest?"

"We promise."

China and Deedee put themselves into high gear. China moved anything heavy. Deedee flipped the plates from the crates to China, who then put them between the plastic teeth. Running to the other side, they reversed the process.

China hated sweat, but she let it roll down her back and her face without trying to mop it off. By three o'clock they'd finished.

Nigel walked around approving. "You ladies have done more than a decent job. You still must fulfill your other duties here at the usual time."

"We know," China said.

"Can we go?" Deedee asked, ready to sprint.

"Yes."

They were gone.

"Where to?" Deedee asked.

"First to the phone. If we can get the police to believe us, we're all done."

"If not?"

"We follow them."

At the infirmary phone, both girls looked at each other. "Do you have money?" China asked Deedee.

"No."

China's energy charge instantly depleted.

"We'll bum some," Deedee said.

"I can't do that."

"Pretend we're teenagers."

"We *are* teenagers," China reminded her.

"I mean ones that bum money all the time."

"You go ahead. I'll stay here and be invisible."

Deedee put on her full charm. She sauntered up to a young couple with three kids hovering about their legs. "Hi, I need change to make an important phone call. Can you help me?"

China pretended she didn't know Deedee. The man dug into his pocket. Seconds later, Deedee ran up to China. "See, it wasn't that hard."

China held out her hand. "Just give it to me." The money jangled as the phone swallowed it. China felt her stomach flip as a woman answered the phone. "Grizzly Peak Police."

China cleared her throat. "May I please speak with a policeman?"

"Would you like us to send an officer out to you?"

The word is officer, you dummy. China hoped the woman hadn't thought she was five years old. "No thank you. Speaking to an officer on the phone would be fine."

It seemed forever that she was on hold. Deedee fidgeted. Chewed her nails. Paced. Folded her arms. Played with her hair.

The moment the officer came on the line, China's mind went blank. All the wonderful adult things she'd been planning to say disappeared. All that was left fell out of her mouth. "There's a kid missing from the camp and I know they found a body and we heard gunshots and I think I know who killed him. It's these two ladies who claim to be riders at this conference, but they've been talking about this murder all along."

"Slow down, slow down. Who is this?"

"China, sir."

"How old are you, China?"

"Fifteen."

"Well, China. I'm sure you mean well, but I think you've been watching too much television. We have the situation under control. There has been no crime committed."

"That's exactly what they want you to think! They're over here celebrating, and you've bought their lies."

"I'll keep that in mind. If we need you, we'll call you."

The phone went dead.

China held the receiver away from her face. She stared at it. "He hung up on me! He didn't believe me."

Deedee shook her head. "It's not like you did a real great job, China."

"You could have done better?"

"Probably not, but I'm just saying . . ."

"Don't say anything." China turned away from the phone, frustrated and angry.

"China," Deedee pleaded.

The phone rang. Both girls watched as it rang again. "Maybe it's the police officer!" Deedee said. "You answer it."

China picked up the phone as if she were a secretary in a formal law firm. "Hello. How may I help you?"

"Yo, babe!" came a nasally voice. "Samuel J. here. Got any stories for me?"

China pressed her lips together and sighed. "Oh yeah. I've got some story, but you wouldn't believe it if I told you. No one else does."

"Try me."

China went through the whole thing, with a little more detail and a whole lot less excitement than what she told the officer. She spoke into the phone, watching to see if anyone heard. The only person close enough to hear was Deedee. But trying to hide behind the tree was good old Walter. She knew he couldn't hear, because the look on his face grew from intense concentration to one of frustration, then anger.

She finished with, "And no one believes there's a murder committed." She wanted to add, "B.T., I'm not kidding." But she wasn't about to blow his little game.

"Hmmm. I'm not surprised. It's not a very plausible story," Mr. Gleckenspiel said. "I think you'll have to come up with something a little stronger. Besides, that's not what I'm looking for. I want stories of camp. You know. Kids. Shenanigans. Stuff other kids can laugh with. Relate to."

China banged on the side of the telephone booth, growling in frustration, then she handed the phone to Deedee.

"Who was the guy who answered the phone yesterday?" Mr. Gleckenspiel asked her.

"What are you talking about?" Deedee said. China stuck her ear next to Deedee's.

"Yesterday you didn't answer the phone. Some guy with a gravelly voice answered instead. He said not to work with you girls because you were thieves. If I wanted some good story material, I should ask him."

China looked over at Walter.

Deedee sighed. "It's just some little old guy at the conference. He keeps rattling on about us being spies for Hollywood or something."

Mr. Gleckenspiel chuckled. "He says he's a great writer and I should see his stuff."

"I doubt it," Deedee said. "All the other riders don't know how to ride."

"What?"

"Even if he really is an old rodeo man, I think he's too old to do what he used to."

Silence greeted her.

"I'll call again tomorrow. See what you can come up with. If I'm going to create this series, I have to have a believable plot to start with."

Deedee replaced the receiver. "I forgot all about Walter."

China jerked her head in the direction of Walter. "He sure didn't."

"I wish B.T. would quit this game. It isn't funny right now."

"I know. But he can't help it. Let's tell him next time he calls as B.T.." She grabbed Deedee's wrist. "Come on. Let's go see Rick."

Deedee's brows wrinkled. "Why do you want to see him now?"

"We have some work to do. He's crucial to Plan B."

It seemed like years since China had worked in the Eelapuash kitchen. The sounds were bright and cheerful as always. As they approached the dining hall, they could hear Rick singing his heart out, the tune bathing the outside of the building with joy.

As soon as China opened the screen door, she felt the peace of the place wash over her. Inside, Rick swooped in, gathered them both in his arms, and danced around and around the kitchen. "I've missed you, my ladies!" He kissed both their hands, making them blush. "Bologna misses you! Why haven't you come to see us?"

"Working in the main kitchen is so different," China said, relieved to be talking to another friend. "We've had to work more hours than usual. It's just work, sleep . . ."

"And worry," Deedee added.

Rick took both Deedee's hands in his. "Worry about what?"

The girls glanced at each other, then shook their heads. "It's too complicated."

"And no one believes us anyway."

"What we need is to borrow something from you

right away," China told him. "We don't have much time. We're ditching work as it is."

Rick frowned. "Magda would be very unhappy if she heard that."

"But she's not going to, is she?" China said.

Rick regarded her out of the corner of his eye. "No, she's not."

"Where is she?" Deedee asked.

"On a break. I've been making her take them in the afternoon." He clapped his hands together. "So, what do you need?"

"Your tape recorder and a blank tape," China said.

Rick shook his head. "I don't know. I don't see you in days and all you want is something precious of mine to break? I don't loan my things out to strangers."

"Come on, Rick," Deedee pleaded. "We'll be your friends forever."

"I thought you were already my friends forever."

"Please?" China said in a small voice.

The girls linked pinkies and cocked their heads.

Rick slapped his forehead. "How can I resist a look like that? Here's my keys. It's on the top of my dresser."

CHAPTER THIRTEEN

BOLOGNA LICKED THEM from head to toe, thrilled to see his masters again. Once they got the tape recorder, China hated pushing him back inside the door and closing it. "Sorry, little guy. We've got serious work to do. We have to save someone else now."

They returned the keys to Rick and dashed off to their hiding place.

"How will we find them?" Deedee asked.

"They always seem to take a walk in the afternoon," China said. "I bet they go right back to our hiding place. They seem to like it there. If they don't show up before it's time for work, we'll try to track them down somewhere else."

China crawled into the hideout, while Deedee waited down the creek a short way. She pretended to read a book, but China could tell it was only pretend. She couldn't believe her eyes when Belina and Marjean showed up within 10 minutes, walking slowly, then sitting on the fallen log. She switched the tape recorder on.

"I'm going to tell them the whole story," Belina was saying.

"And risk everything?" Marjean asked.

"Well, it's because of this conference that it all turned out so well. Without what I learned in class, I don't know that I could have come up with a workable solution so quickly."

"I wouldn't do it. I would hate to see the table turned on you."

"I don't think that will happen. I think the skit and the awards ceremony would be the perfect place to do it."

"I don't think they'd understand, Belina. You have to be real careful what you say in a place like this."

Deedee walked casually up to the women. "Hi! I wondered how everything is going."

"Great!" Belina smiled. "I'm sorry I got so mad at you guys. I was just under a lot of pressure to get something difficult done. But it's over now, and I think I can be more civil."

China was amazed that Deedee could make such a forced smile look natural.

"I heard you killed Harrison."

"You did? Well, it wasn't easy. But I did it."

"When?"

"Yesterday. I cried through the whole thing. But when it was over, I knew I had done the right thing and that I did a good job of it."

"How did you do it?" Deedee's eyes flashed fear, but the rest of her stayed calm.

"Well, we had to get him up to that old mine shaft. It actually wasn't that difficult. All we had to do was tell him a couple of the boys were trapped up there." Belina's face got very soft. "He always was a softie for kids. He'd do anything for them. That's why he wanted out. To help the kids."

"How did you actually kill him?"

"One of the leaders pushed him over the edge of the mine." She sighed. "He didn't even scream going down."

"So you didn't actually push him?"

Belina regarded her. "In a way I did, didn't I?"

Deedee shook her head. "I don't know how you could do that."

"It's not something I ever really wanted to do. But in this business you have to do some things you'd rather not. Whatever brings in the money is sometimes all that counts."

Deedee swallowed hard. "How do you pronounce your name?"

China rolled her eyes. She knew Deedee had to get Belina to say her name on the tape so it would be verified who the person was.

"Buh-leena," Belina said slowly. "Belina Sarcona."

Deedee stood. "I need to go now. Congratulations on doing what you felt you had to do."

She turned to walk away and Marjean put a hand

on her arm. Deedee shivered noticeably in the heat. "Why don't you guys come to the skit and awards ceremony tonight? You might be able to better understand what we do."

"Thanks," Deedee said halfheartedly.

Belina and Marjean stood and walked toward the creek. Deedee walked the opposite way on the trail, looking back often. When they were out of sight, China burrowed her way outside.

"We've got it!" China shouted.

Deedee came close and said, sadly, "I thought I'd feel better about it, but I don't."

Heavy, lumbering footsteps approached.

China took a crumpled piece of paper out of her pocket and wrapped it around the cassette tape, adding a rubber band to hold it together. In a hurried whisper, she told Deedee, "We'll get Rick to take the cassette to the police. I wrote a note that tells them this tape is proof a murder has taken place. And that we don't know how to find the ladies—I mean, women —unless they come to the meeting tonight."

In a moment the footsteps would be upon them. China's heart beat faster. Deedee looked around to see who might be coming. She spoke fast. "What do you make of her saying they pushed him into the mine, yet they still found a body?"

China shook her head. "Maybe there was a bottom to the hole and he rolled out of it."

"STOP!"

China and Deedee looked up from their task. Walter stood there, ape-like, his arms held in curves away from his body. He breathed in huffs. "You ain't goin' nowhere with that tape. I know what you're going to do with it. An' I ain't gonna allow it. I'm gonna take it to the head honcho of this place. And I'm gonna tell him what you two have been up to."

"Look," Deedee pleaded. "We're trying to take care of something that really isn't your business."

"It is too my business, because ultimately it affects me." Walter swayed back and forth, heavy breaths still coming from his mouth. With one motion, swifter than China or Deedee thought he could move, Walter leapt forward. He snatched the tape and ran over the creek bridge.

China deftly ran over the fallen pine tree to beat him to the other side.

As China stood in front of Walter, he moved his hand behind him to keep the tape from her reach. He danced and pranced to try to get around her, but China moved faster. She tried to reach around him to get the tape. She knew it was hopeless, but wanted to keep him focused on her. The ploy worked. Deedee snuck up behind, grabbing the tape from Walter's hand.

She took off running up the hill and into the forest. She couldn't run terribly fast with her hiking boots, but no one was any match for her knowledge of the forest. Walter ran after her while China dropped to sit on a rock. She knew the tape would get to Rick safely.

Within minutes, Walter returned, breathless. "I'm not done with you yet, Missy. I'm gonna make certain everyone knows what kind of person you are."

"You do that," China said. "I'd really like everyone to know."

Walter hitched his way over the bridge and disappeared at the bend in the trail. China stuck her feet in the cool water and tossed rocks in while waiting for Deedee. When Deedee returned, she told China that Rick took the tape with the solemn promise he would deliver it to the police within the hour that Magda returned. He promised not tell anyone about it. He also promised he would not look at the note.

"He promised?" China asked.

"Well, he actually said he'd do the best he could. But he wasn't sure he could get a break before dinner. They're short handed too, since you're not there."

"We can't count on him then."

"I've been trying to think of other ways we can prove the murder, but I haven't figured one out yet."

China threw one last rock into the water. It landed like a period on the end of a sentence. "We'll think of something."

Walking back to main camp, China felt like someone had unplugged her. "I'm so whooped. I feel like I haven't slept in a week."

"Maybe you haven't," Deedee said. "My dreams have been doozies these days."

As they passed the Administration building, a

woman came charging out the door. "Deedee! Wait! Your dad wants to talk to you for a minute."

Deedee's eyebrows raised. To China she said, "Maybe he's come to his senses."

Mr. Kiersey's office was not one that held pleasant memories for China. She didn't think she would ever forget Heather's false accusation that China had stolen money. She had almost been sent home from camp. She sat in the same old leather chair that had held her when she was in trouble. Mr. Kiersey put his hand up. "I only have a moment. I'm supposed to be on my way out. We still haven't found that high school kid."

Deedee opened her mouth, but Mr. Kiersey stopped her. "We've got more trouble brewing in the kitchen. I've just had word from a conferee that one or two of the kitchen workers are up to something funny. It was intimated that we may have something very serious taking place there. I would like you girls to watch and listen and see what you can find out. Okay?"

The girls looked at each other. *Glenda,* they both mouthed.

"Daddy," Deedee said. "I think I know who it is."

"Just listen for tonight. Don't make any snap judgments. You know I prefer to have all the facts. I never like to unfairly accuse anyone."

"If it is the person I'm thinking about, it could be something you might want to tell the police."

Mr. Kiersey nodded. "That's what my impression was. But whatever damage has been done has been done already. I don't want to make any false accusations. The person reporting said he didn't know the names. He refused to point out the problem people just yet. He told me it was my job to control my workers and hire reputable people. Now, if you girls will excuse me, I think you need to get back to work, and I need to continue organizing a search team for this kid."

"Is it Harrison?" Deedee asked.

"You heard."

"Try the old mine off the horse trail," Deedee said.

"Great idea. Kids tend to be drawn to that mine."

"Or lured there," China said under her breath.

"What about the body they found?" Deedee asked. "Maybe that's Harrison?"

"What body? Who found it? Why wasn't I told?"

"I guess the rangers found it. That's all I know."

"I'd better call immediately."

Out the door, China turned to Deedee. "My heart *aches* for Harrison."

"Mine too."

"Did you hear what your dad said? He said problem *people*. One or two kitchen workers. That must mean there's more than one person in on this with Glenda."

As the kitchen came into view, Deedee said, "What do you think she's up to?"

"I think she's in with Marjean and Belina. Maybe they're all part of this secret group."

"We'd better be extra careful," Deedee said. "They don't think twice about killing people who get in their way."

China shook her head. "They think twice about it, but they don't think three times."

Deedee and China emerged from the pit as if they'd been there all afternoon. As they asked Glenda for instructions, she again gave them options about what they could do to help food preparations. Whatever she offered, the girls always chose the task that would keep them closest to her so they could watch and listen. But the only thing they could gather was her continual distaste for them.

"Maybe it's not her," Deedee said to China, when Glenda went to get more potato flakes.

"It has to be her," China said. "There's hardly anyone left in the kitchen. They're all sick."

"Two have come back," Deedee reminded her.

"But barely. No one would have the chance to complain about them."

"I wish we knew what the complaint was."

All through serving dinner, China shook. Her hands shook. Her knees shook. Her voice shook when she offered to bring more mashed potatoes. Her stomach was so nervous she couldn't eat when it was time to take a break. Her body often seemed to be her enemy rather than her friend, like now.

At least the "riders" were nicer to her. Whatever confusing misunderstandings Walter had against them about being "spies for Hollywood" must have dissipated. For he seemed happy. In fact, he seemed too happy. He chuckled to himself all meal long, eating so much that China was afraid he'd pop. He was muttering about justice being just around the corner and something about someone finally listening to him and taking him seriously.

I wish someone would listen to us, China thought. *I wonder who he talked to. Maybe I should ask so we can be taken seriously too.*

Walter nodded at her and smiled so often that it was creepy. Marjean and Belina commented on what a nice chat they'd had with Deedee in the afternoon. "I wish you could have been there," Belina told her. "I think we got some things straightened out."

China smiled. "That's what I heard. Everything is very clear now."

Marjean said, "Did your friend tell you that you're invited to come tonight?"

"We'll be there for sure," China told her.

At the end of dinner, Walter grabbed her arm. "It's all over now," he said with glee.

"Yes," China agreed, "dinner is over."

Walter tittered like a little kid. "It's all over and you'll find justice right around the corner. You'll have yours, and I'll have mine. And I can finally sleep at night knowing you're taken care of."

China felt her face contort into a *What is he talking about?* look. "I really think Walter's losing whatever marbles he had left," she told Deedee inside the swinging doors. She looked around to see if anyone was listening. "Have you heard anything?"

"Glenda's been acting really strange. She told me Lori's almost well. When I told her that was great, she gave me one of those evil looks and said, 'You *would* think that, wouldn't you?'"

"I think this whole place has been taken over by aliens," China said. "I don't think there's any other explanation for it."

"That's not all."

China peeked out the window in the swinging door. "It'll have to wait. Both our tables need coffee."

China's stomach gurgled like a percolating coffee pot. She hoped it would stay where it belonged and not embarrass her.

The "riders" finally left, allowing the girls to clean off the tables. In the midst of all the clatter, they could talk without fear of being overheard.

"I heard Glenda talking to Jennifer," Deedee told China. "She said she's sure it's going to happen soon."

"What's going to happen?"

"I don't know."

China wiped her hands on her apron, then picked up another plate to scrape garbage into a large serving bowl. Deedee gathered the silverware.

"That's not much help," China said, looking around at the other waitresses also clearing tables.

"This is." Deedee looked around again. "She said as soon as the kitchen clears out, she'll tell her."

"We've got to nail something here, Deeds. I'm tired of all this spooky stuff going on and no one believing us. I say we stay here and listen."

They moved to the next table, starting their routine all over again.

"I agree. But how can we listen without them knowing?"

China smiled. "I know just the place."

CHAPTER FOURTEEN

THE GIRLS WASHED the evening dishes as quickly as they had the ones at lunch.

Nigel raised his eyebrows. "I think I'm going to put in for you two as permanent staff."

"It's very kind of you." Deedee said. "But please don't."

"You are the *best* workers."

"Can we go now?" China asked, anxious to hear what Glenda had planned.

"Yes, you are excused. Will you be going to the skit tonight? I hear it's going to be quite funny."

"If we go now, we can probably get there on time," China said a little too eagerly.

"Then go, go," Nigel said.

China grabbed Deedee's hand and practically dragged her up the rubber-covered stairs. She punched a button. When the stainless steel doors opened like silver jaws, she told Deedee, "Get in."

"You *are* kidding," Deedee said. "I'm not getting into that thing."

"You can hear everything without anyone knowing you're here. Come on. We have to. This is your chance to prove to your father that all this stuff we've been trying to tell him is not crazy. Now shush and get in."

The nearly empty kitchen lay silent and shining after thorough scrubbing. Deedee looked around.

"Get in before someone sees us," China begged.

"You first."

"Uhhh!" China groaned. "Fine." She scrambled into the dumbwaiter and made herself as small as she could.

"There's no more room," Deedee whined.

China struggled to make herself even smaller.

"I'll just wait out here. I'll hide in a cupboard or something."

"You are impossible!" China reached out, grabbed Deedee's wrist, and gave a yank.

Deedee fell forward and caught herself on the edge of the stainless steel box. "Okay, okay. Just give me a minute."

"We haven't got a minute."

Voices approached from the back room. "It's Glenda!" Deedee whispered. The voice was enough to make her get into the box. China reached out and pushed the button for the door to close, letting the dumbwaiter stay where it was. As the doors slid shut, it was like a microphone turned on. Glenda's voice rang loud and clear.

"Lori's better. That means we have to confront

Rahja pretty soon. His actions against Lori are unfounded and unfair."

"Deedee, your hair's in my mouth," China whispered, trying not to cough.

"Sorry."

Deedee unclipped her hair, gathered it all together behind her head and reinstalled the clip.

"Do you really think he's out to hurt Lori?"

"It sure looks that way. He practically admitted it to me himself."

"That doesn't sound like him."

"He's got you fooled too, huh? Well if you heard what I heard . . ."

"You were eavesdropping?"

"Not really. But Rahja didn't know I could hear everything he was saying."

"How do you know you heard right?"

Glenda sputtered. "It was obvious. Anyway, I think it's all going to happen when Lori gets back. And I want your support. I want you to tell him everything you know. I want those two gone for good."

"And we want to be gone, thank you very much," Deedee whispered to China.

China put her finger to her lips. *What if they mean "gone for good" as in giving them the old heave-ho into an abandoned mine shaft?* China wondered. She looked at Deedee and drew her finger across her throat. Deedee's eyes grew wide.

"I don't think they're so bad."

"But if they don't go, there will be no room for Lori."

Jennifer's voice then came from a different part of their listening box. *She must have moved to another part of the kitchen,* China thought.

"What do you want me to do?"

"I don't really know yet. I need your help on that. They've messed things up so bad . . ."

"Why don't we ask those writer people, Belina and Marjean? They seem to come up with real good ideas."

"Good idea, Jen. If they can figure out a clean murder in a couple days, they ought to have this solved in no time." China could hear approval in Glenda's voice.

"You shouldn't tell them what you plan to do, Glenda. It's not really ethical."

"True. I'll think of something. But don't tell anyone. Don't even tell Lori."

"She doesn't know?"

"She really needs this job. I didn't want to worry her. Especially when she was so sick."

"I hope I can help," Jennifer said. "But I don't want to lie to Rahja or do anything else wrong."

Glenda's voice rose. "I thought you were my friend."

"I am. But I refuse to hurt two innocent people for anyone."

Good for you.

"They aren't innocent. I caught them . . ." Glenda's voice trailed off. "Never mind. I'm not at liberty to say."

Because you'll get yourself in trouble for being in the file room, China thought.

"I'd better find Belina and Marjean," Glenda said. "I heard through the grapevine they're winning awards tonight. I want to find them before then. They'll be too excited afterwards. I know *they'll* help me."

Footsteps made little tapping sounds in the metal behind China's head. Then all was silent.

"Deedee. Would you please get your hair out of my mouth?"

"Sorry." Deedee pulled her hair back again, refastening it in the large clip. "It seems to have a mind of its own." She patted her head. "So, how do we get out of here?"

"Why do you say it like that? We just open the doors and leave. Simple."

"The doors aren't like elevator doors, China."

"Deeds. What's the prob? You're sounding a little crabby."

"You would be too if you were stuck in a tiny box all wadded up like a used tissue."

"I am. I even have a phobia about this kind of thing. But I'm trying to be a big girl and be brave."

"Well, be brave then when I tell you the doors don't open automatically."

China's mouth popped open. "But they opened when I rode it before."

"That's because Glenda pushed the button."

China looked around the dark little box, her head whipping from side to side. All she could see was a jumble of arms and legs tossed together with two bodies.

"Pfff," Deedee muffled a laugh. "You aren't looking for an inside button, are you?"

"Everything in the kitchen is fitted with safety features," China said.

"This was meant for food and dishes. Dishes do not have fingers. At least not the last time I looked. This was definitely not meant for *people*."

"Or two dumb girls."

"One dumb girl, and one idiot who does what the dumb girl tells her to," Deedee huffed. "I can't believe I ever listen to you. You get us into the most insane positions."

"Me?" shrieked China. "You're the one who lives in this nuthouse they call a camp. I've never had stuff like this happen to me before."

"Oh, I'll bet."

"Why don't we just yell? Maybe someone will hear us."

"And how would we explain this?" Deedee asked. "Besides, I think everyone has gone home."

Both girls pondered their predicament.

"My whole body has gone numb," Deedee complained.

"Well I have a solution. Stretch your muscles. You can begin by moving your hand. I'm tired of it being in front of my mouth."

"My hand is not in front of your mouth."

"Is too."

"Is not."

"Move it or I'll bite it." The hand didn't move. So China opened her mouth, moved forward, and chomped.

"OWWW!"

Deedee shook her head. "I told you it wasn't my hand."

China sucked on her hand where she'd bit it. "How was I supposed to tell? It's so dark in here."

"No, duh. You think they put lights in little dark boxes for food? Food doesn't care."

"Then why do they put lights in refrigerators? Huh? Just answer that one if you think you're so smart."

Deedee stared through the dark at China. "They put lights in refrigerators for the people who open the door."

"No. Really?"

"China?"

"Yeah?"

"Are you losing your mind?"

"I never had one to lose."

Deedee sighed. "Great. Now you tell me."

"Since I've lost my mind . . ."

"That you never had to lose in the first place . . ."

"Why don't you get us out of here."

"ME?" Deedee shrieked.

"Yes, you. You're the one who's lived here all your life. You probably know all the secret ways to get out of anything."

"That's what you think. We're stuck," Deedee announced.

"Really? I hadn't noticed."

"It's also very cramped in here."

"You are coming up with some startling revelations, Deeds. Maybe you should be a prophet."

"You were the one who found your way out of a walk-in refrigerator, China. That means you've had experience. The person with lesser experience always defers to the one who has more."

China was silent.

"Well?"

"I hate it when you're right."

Deedee shifted.

WHUMP!

The dumbwaiter slipped and dropped a few inches.

"What was that?" China asked.

"I don't want to know," Deedee said.

China breathed real shallow and held very still.

WHUMP!

The tiny box slipped again.

"Don't look now, Deedee Kiersey. But we're falling down an elevator shaft."

CHAPTER FIFTEEN

"CHINA. IT'S NOT LIKE the elevator shaft goes for fifty floors."

"One floor or fifty, we could still die."

"We're not going to die."

"Not yet. But we will for sure after the hit squad gets hold of us."

"That was a weird conversation between Glenda and Jennifer, wasn't it?"

"Most conversations this week have been weird. Has there been one normal one at all?"

"It didn't make much sense," Deedee said to herself, as if she hadn't heard a word China said.

"Sure it did. Glenda wants to get rid of us. And she's asking the murderers to help."

"How do you know it's us she's talking about?" Deedee said.

"Isn't it rather obvious? She's hated us all week for no reason."

WHUMP!

125

"Can we stay on one subject, please?" China asked. "I think we should focus on getting out of this box before we fall and die."

"We're not going to fall and die. We'd suffocate first."

"Now that's a happy thought." China sputtered. "Your hair's in my mouth again."

"Sorry." Deedee started to laugh. "No matter what we do, we're going to die. So which way do you suggest we do it? Suffocate? Fall? Be pushed into a mine shaft?"

"Then we'd get to meet Harrison again," China said cheerfully.

"He was kinda cute," Deedee added.

"Kinda? He was incredibly cute."

WHUMP!

"Uh," China said. "How many more whumps do you think it will take before we hit bottom?"

"Sounds like a Dr. Seuss rhyme book. 'How many flumps do whumps crump plump?'"

"Do you have a screwdriver?" China asked.

"Oh yeah. I carry one with me everywhere I go."

China smiled. "You're right! You do! Give me your hair clip."

Deedee unfastened her hair clip and handed it to China.

"Deeds. Really. How many whumps do you think it would take to reach bottom?"

"Why is this question necessary?"

"Because I don't know whether I should drop us out of the bottom or whether we should climb out of the top. Which end are we closer to? To the bottom or the top?"

"If we go out the top, we'd still have the bottom of this thing to stand on. If we try to go out the bottom, we'll have nothing to stand on if it's too far."

"Good point."

China felt over her head for the screws she hoped would be there. "I can't get these, Deedee. You do the ones over my head, and then I'll do the ones over yours."

Deedee took the hair clip and put the thin metal end into the screw. "Which way do I turn?"

"Lefty-loosie, Righty-tighty."

"Well, isn't that a handy little saying."

"Deedee. Just turn it to the left."

Deedee's arm covered China's eyes. Her hand kept slipping, causing her elbow to collide with China's nose. China hoped no permanent damage would be done. "Can you hurry, Deeds? The smell I'm getting here isn't incredibly pleasant."

"The thing isn't moving. It's in too tight."

"Weakling," China muttered.

Deedee dropped the clip onto China's head. "You do it then, Amazon Woman."

"Okay, I will." China reached over Deedee's head and found a screw.

China stuck the clip end into the screw and turned

it slowly but firmly. Nothing happened. She positioned the clip better and tried again. Still nothing. She put more force behind the turn. Then the clip snapped.

WHUMP!

"Now, what?" Deedee asked. "Got another brilliant idea?"

Both girls grew quiet, thinking of what they could do. China kept getting distracted by her cramped muscles and dripping sweat. The stench of rotted food wafted stronger, if possible.

She tried to stretch her cramped arm, catching Deedee's nose with her fingernail. "Sorry."

Deedee shifted and caught China's backside with her foot. "Double sorry."

WHUMP!

"I bet we're almost to the bottom now," China said. "Maybe we should just sleep here and wait until someone needs to use the dumbwaiter in the morning."

"Why not pry the door open?"

"I thought we already discussed that."

"I just said the doors didn't open automatically."

China sputtered. "Why didn't you say that earlier, before we started whumping our way down? We could have been out of here a long time ago."

"Don't get too depressed. It might not work now."

"Which way do the doors open on this thing?"

"The outside door pulls up, and the inside door slides down."

China moved her fingers around the door, trying to find where it might begin. A sharp piece of turned metal caught the edge of her finger. "Ouch!" She sucked on the bleeding wound. "Here's where we have to get it open." She guided Deedee's hand gently to the spot.

Both girls tried to get their fingers into the crack and push down on the door.

"What I wouldn't give for Heather's long nails right now," Deedee said.

"What we need is a credit card."

"Too bad I left mine at home," Deedee teased.

"You know the saying," China told her, "American Express . . . never leave home without it."

For the next few moments, they shifted and moved, trying to find something to put in the small slit and make the door pop open.

WHUMP!

"What if we just push against the door?" Deedee suggested.

"It won't work," China told her.

Deedee wiped her hands off on her shorts, then put her palms flat on the metal. She pushed down.

The door opened.

"Well, now, that was terribly difficult," Deedee said.

"Okay, smarty pants. What next?"

"There's the other door," Deedee pointed.

They could barely see the top part.

"We need one more whump to get out," China suggested.

"Okay," Deedee said brightly. She shifted and bounced until the dumbwaiter complied. WHUMP!

They couldn't reach the bottom of the door as easily to push it up. But the top curved in a nice handle. "I give you the honor," Deedee indicated to China.

"No, you," China said. "You were the one who had complete faith."

Deedee put her fingers underneath the metal lip and pushed up.

Nothing happened. The door stayed still.

"Great," China moaned. "Just great."

Both girls put their fingers into the lip and pushed. It wouldn't budge.

"Wait a sec," China said. "Look." She pointed to a piece of plastic blocking the way of the door opening.

"Oh, that's right," Deedee said. "This thing has been sticking sometimes. I bet that's why." She twisted the plastic until it finally broke off. The door opened easily after that.

Deedee wiggled around until she could squeeze out the hole feet first. China pushed on her shoulders to help her wiggle out.

For China to get out, Deedee had to grab hold of her feet and pull. "I always wondered what it felt like to be born," she told Deedee.

"I thought it was more like Winnie the Pooh getting stuck in the hole after eating too much honey."

"Are you saying I'm fat?"

"Hardly."

China slapped her forehead. "We really *are* stupid."

"Why?"

"After you got out, you could have pushed the button for the dumbwaiter to come all the way down. I didn't need to squeeze out."

Deedee grinned real big. "I know that."

"What—?"

"I didn't think I should be the only one to have to suffer and squeeze out that tiny hole."

China kicked her playfully. "I don't know why I let you be my friend."

"Let me?"

China smiled.

Deedee checked her watch. "Uh-oh. The meeting has already started."

China got serious real fast. "We've got to let everyone know what Belina and Marjean have done. They don't deserve an award."

"We look awful."

"Speak for yourself."

"Actually, I was speaking for you. You've got something green hanging from your hair."

China felt her hair until she found the slimy old piece of broccoli clinging for dear life.

"So we're going to stand up in front of all these people and in our own stinky way say these people are scumbags?" Deedee asked.

"I think that's the only way we can get them cornered into admitting what they've done. Or even see what they did was wrong. I don't think the other riders will stand for impostors. They won't let them get away with it."

"What proof do we have to convince anyone?"

"Deeds! Look!" China pointed into the shaft. A dirty ball of paper sat in the dark, rear corner. She took two steps and reached her arm deep into the slime of old food. "Now we've got our proof. Let's go. Before it's too late."

CHAPTER SIXTEEN

DEEDEE AND CHINA FLUNG OPEN the side door to the meeting hall and marched toward the front. A very tall, skinny man with very little hair was speaking into the microphone. "The writing award for adults goes to . . . Belina Sarcona; and for children, Marjean Kenilworth."

"No!" China shouted.

"Wait!" Deedee said at the same moment.

"Stop!" they said together.

"They don't deserve these awards," China said loudly, "They can't ride at all!"

"We were on the horses behind them," Deedee added. "They were awful!"

The crowd roared with laughter. "Good thing you don't make your living at that!" someone called out.

"You think this is *funny?*" China said to the crowd, mounting the steps to the stage. "This woman plotted and carried out a murder this week. And this one helped. On Monday they heard they had to do it, and they completed it either last night or early this morning."

The crowd stood and cheered. "Yeah! Go Belina!"

Belina looked like someone had taken the wind out of her. "*I* wanted to tell them that. That was *my* story."

China looked at Deedee, her mouth open wide enough to catch a 747. "This whole place has gone nuts. They're *applauding* her!"

"We have proof!" Deedee pleaded, waving the paper over her head. "In her own handwriting . . . she wrote it all down. From start to finish."

China leaned into the microphone. "And even what things she decided not to do. It shows she thought long and hard about what she was going to do and how she was going to do it."

"It was premeditated," Deedee said.

"Make copies!" someone in the crowd shouted.

"We want to see how the pros do it!" shouted another.

China put her hand to her throat and choked. "I can't believe it. They're all very, very sick. I want to get out of here."

The emcee took the papers from the girls and looked them over. "It's true. This is Belina's handwriting."

"They stole those from me," Belina said quietly. "Not that it really matters any more. But I would like to reclaim my property."

China put her hand between the emcee and Belina. "You're not going to give all the proof over to her, are you?"

"It is her creation. By law it belongs to her."

"But she managed to complete a murder this week!" Deedee protested.

The emcee spoke into the mike again. "I talked to Belina on the first day. She told me she'd just received an urgent phone call. The murder had to be done and had to be completed by Friday. She didn't miss a class, and she still managed to do what was required of her and do an excellent job. And this is why we want to give her an award. She is a great example to all of us—whether we are just beginning or have been writing a long time."

"I think this is horrible," Deedee said.

"Rotten," said China.

"This is a tough business for outsiders to understand," said the emcee. "Why don't you have a seat and watch our skit, *Little Red Writing Hood*. Perhaps it will help you to grasp the concepts we have to deal with every day."

"I don't know if I want to understand," China muttered. "*Little Red Riding Hood* is about a cannibalistic wolf who devours a sweet granny. There ya have it. Murder again. In cold blood. With nothing left. I didn't know killing people was what riding is all about."

"Ahh, but who's the hero in the end?" the emcee said. "Who actually comes out on top? Little Red Writing Hood. Go on. Sit down. Enjoy the skit. You might learn something. Even if you don't, it will be fun to watch."

"Fun?" China said, as she walked down the stairs. "I think I'm going to be sick."

"Me, too," said Deedee.

China led Deedee to the front row. "If I'm supposed to understand this, I want to sit smack dab in front." They slid into the pew, going all the way to the center of the row. Deedee sunk low into her seat. China sat straight and tall, her hands folded in her lap.

The lights dimmed. Music started. Silly music, from way back. Some wolf howled a lot and they sang about Little Red Writing Hood. While the music played, some ditzy woman skipped and twirled down the aisle, blowing bubbles.

"She must be Little Red Riding Hood," Deedee whispered.

"Her hood's pink," China said.

"So she's Little Pink Riding Hood."

On stage, a stone-faced woman held up signs in her hands. One said, "Publishing House Way." The other said, "Forest Road."

As the Hood reached the stage, a tall man dressed in a poorly fitted, ugly maroon, polyester suit with a fox tail dangling from the seat of his pants appeared on the scene. Tall furry ears bounced with every step. The crowd roared.

The Wolf wound his way around the Hood, cooing and talking to her about . . .

"A *manuscript?*" Deedee said, slowly sitting up in the chair. "What are they talking about?"

"Oh, my publisher is looking forward to my new book manuscript being done," Hood said brightly.

"A *book* manuscript?" Deedee's voice got tiny and pinched.

"Oooh," cooed the Wolf. "I'd love to eat, I mean read your manuscript."

The Wolf slammed into the Hood and sent her and her manuscript flying. He spun the sign around so the Hood would take the wrong path to her publisher. Then he helped her up and sent her on her way.

China felt a shiver run up her spine, and color start to edge into her cheeks. She didn't dare look to one side or the other. She didn't dare even look at Deedee.

As the skit went on, the Hood encountered various plagues and people and beings who were determined to take her manuscript from her. When she found the Wolf again, and discovered who he was, she stood up and said, "I worked long and hard writing this book! And I'm not going to let you steal it now."

China felt the red edging up her face in full tidal waves of color and heat. She sank down in her seat. Lower and lower and lower.

"They're *writers*," Deedee was saying over and over. "They're *writers*, not *riders*."

"I wish I could be a puddle on the floor," mumbled China. "Become invisible. Something. Anything. Anything but China Jasmine Tate, the ultimate fool."

The crowd stood and cheered. The cast came out and bowed. And China and Deedee covered their faces in total embarrassment. Deedee finally leaned over to China. Without uncovering much of her face she whispered. "Now I know what 'my most embarrassing moment' is."

"Writers! Deedee. WRITERS! How could we be so *stupid?*"

Belina slipped in beside the girls. "Do you understand now? When the publisher says you do something, you do it. When your editor is going to make changes for you, you never know how it's going to turn out. They sometimes know what's best. And sometimes they make a mistake. But for the most part, a writer has to realize the editors often see important flaws in our work that we don't."

"So Harrison isn't a real person?" Deedee asked.

China nudged her sharply to be quiet.

Belina's brows pulled together. "Why no. He's a character I created . . ." She paused, then her brows lifted and her eyes and voice filled with laughter. "You didn't. You thought Harrison was *real?* You thought I killed a real person?"

Deedee nodded and China nudged her harder this time.

"How awful for you! No wonder you guys were crazy about this murder thing." Belina put back her head and laughed in a very loud, very un-petite way. Marjean fell in behind them, heard the story, and joined in. Within moments everyone within five rows knew the story and added to the girls' total humiliation.

"I can't stand this," China groaned.

"Nothing worse could happen," Deedee said. "At least this is as bad as it's going to get."

China tried to nod. She hated seeing the tears of glee pouring down Belina's cheeks. She wished, right then, that she could die.

Out of nowhere, a loud squawk filled the air. "ALL RIGHT," came a voice over a bullhorn. "NOBODY MOVE."

The laughter in the room ceased immediately as if flicked off by a light switch.

"THIS IS THE POLICE. WE'VE GOT YOU SUR-ROUNDED. NO ONE IS TO LEAVE UNTIL WE HAVE, IN CUSTODY, A SUSPECT WHO HAS COMMITTED A FELONY."

China and Deedee groaned in unison. "It's worse," China said to Deedee. "This is much worse."

"Now I wish they'd killed *us*," Deedee said.

"They might."

All eyes focused on China and Deedee. Belina's grew extra wide. "What did you do?" she demanded in a loud whisper.

"We taped your confession," Deedee said.

"And turned it over to the police," added China.

CHAPTER SEVENTEEN

MOMENTS LATER, a contingent of what seemed like a million police stormed the room. They burst through every door and stood sentry, hands on their guns.

"Oh, great," China said. "This is just great."

"Down here!" a voice shouted. "They're down here!"

All heads turned toward the voice. Walter hitched himself down the aisle, waving his arms. "I knew you'd come. I knew you'd see the seriousness of what these girls have done."

An officer approached him. "Are you the one who sent the tape?"

"Why, no. Didn't the head boss guy call you?"

"No. We received a tape."

China desperately wanted to crawl under the pew. But the horror of the whole thing kept her glued to her seat.

Mr. Kiersey appeared. "I'm sorry, officer, I think there must be a mistake."

"Sir," Walter said to Mr. Kiersey. "There's no mistake. The kitchen workers are here. They're trying to break up this conference and cause a ruckus. I say they get hauled away before they do more damage."

The police officer pulled a notepad from his back pocket. "We have a tape with a confession to a murder on it. Someone being pushed down an old mine shaft."

"He wasn't pushed," Mr. Kiersey said. "He was a typical high school kid. He went exploring on his own, fell, and broke his foot."

Deedee jumped to her feet. "Harrison?"

"Yes, Harrison."

"Harrison?" Belina said. "There's actually a Harrison?"

"At the old mine?" Marjean asked, incredulously.

Mr. Kiersey nodded. "We found him an hour ago."

"So a crime has been committed," the police officer said. The other officers reacted by unclipping their gun holsters.

"No, no crime has been committed," Mr. Kiersey said.

"Yes there has," Walter said. "These girls are stealing the hard-earned stories of writers and selling them to Hollywood publishers."

Glenda jumped up from her seat. "And they're trying to unlawfully take the place of my friend Lori in the kitchen. I caught them tampering with employee files to falsify information."

"So that's why she was in the file room," Deedee mouthed to China.

China still felt in total shock. She couldn't say a word. The whole mess was completely astounding.

The police officer was writing madly in his little notebook. "Theft of ideas," he said under his breath as he wrote. "Unlawful job stealing. Snooping of employee files."

"What were *you* doing in the file room?" Mr. Kiersey asked Glenda. "How did you get in? We keep that under lock and alarm."

Glenda turned red. The officer looked between the two of them. "Breaking and entering," he wrote. "Who committed the murder?"

Everyone pointed to Belina. "She did."

"But she didn't."

"It was only in a book."

"She made it up. It was pretend."

"Harrison?" Belina kept repeating. "There really was a Harrison here?"

"You Belina Sarcona?" the police officer asked.

"What about the dead body?" Deedee blurted. "Where did the dead body come from?"

"Physical evidence," the officer wrote on his pad.

Belina turned pasty white. If she hadn't been sitting down, she probably would have fainted. "There was a dead body, too?"

Marjean put her hand over her mouth.

"It wasn't Harrison, was it?" Belina said, her eyes brimming with tears.

Mr. Kiersey spoke. "No. Harrison only broke his

foot. The hermit is dead."

"What hermit?" the officer asked. "How come I haven't heard about this yet?"

"The rangers contacted the county sheriff. The body was found outside the jurisdiction of the police department."

The officer looked at him, his pen held high as if wondering whether or not to believe him. "But it was still murder," the officer said.

"No. He most likely died of natural causes. He was very old and obviously dehydrated and malnourished."

"What about Lori?" Glenda shouted. "She shouldn't be terminated due to false accusations."

"What about my stolen ideas?" Walter demanded. He marched up to Mr. Kiersey. "You've got the guilty parties right here. Why don't you do something about it?"

"So was a murder committed or not?" the officer asked. He popped the end of his pen into his mouth and began to chew.

"NOT," chorused the writers.

"No one committed a murder," sighed Mr. Kiersey.

"I'd like to speak with the person who made the tape," the officer announced. "I want to hear it from her own mouth."

China and Deedee both stood.

"That's them!" Walter shouted, pointing. "The spies."

"The intruders who are going to steal Lori's job," Glenda added.

Mr. Kiersey dropped to a pew. He pounded his forehead with the palm of his hand. "What next? What next?"

The doors behind the sentry officers burst open. Three photographers entered, light bulbs flashing. A fourth person, a bearded, casually dressed man with a greasy ponytail marched in behind them. "We're from the *Star World Enterprise* tabloid," he announced. "We have an appointment to talk with . . . " he consulted a paper in his hand, ". . . a Miss Deedee Kiersey and a Miss China Tate."

CHAPTER EIGHTEEN

IF CHINA DIDN'T KNOW the meaning of pande-
monium before, she certainly did now. The room
filled to overflowing with voices, arguments, and
laughter. Mr. Kiersey put up his hand. "ENOUGH!"
When all had quieted down, he said, "I am the Director here. I will take over. No one will speak unless I
give them permission. Clear?"

He turned to China and Deedee. "Girls? Will you
please answer the officer?"

"There was no murder," China said meekly.

"Filing a false report," the officer said as he wrote.

"Why did you say there was?" Mr. Kiersey asked.

"We really thought they were planning to murder
Harrison."

"I told you girls not to worry. That kind of thing was
part of their job. Why didn't you listen to me?"

"I thought you said they were a group of *riders,* not
writers."

Mr. Kiersey rolled his eyes. His fingers started to do

rapid spider push-ups off each other. He looked at the officer. "See. There you have it. There has been no murder. Only a misunderstanding." He looked fiercely at the girls. "And the crime of eavesdropping."

The officer looked disappointed. "Do you want to press other charges?"

"I do!" shouted Walter.

Mr. Kiersey silenced him with a look. "No. Thank you. We know where to find you if we need you. You may go now."

The officers shuffled out of the room to the sound of whirring cameras.

Mr. Kiersey looked over the crowd of eager listeners. "I would ask you all to leave, but it seems as though there has been quite a bit of misunderstanding going on. If you can remain quiet, I will let you stay to hear the explanations."

He motioned for Walter to come sit next to him. "Are these the two workers you suspected of acting strangely?" Mr. Kiersey asked, indicating Deedee and China.

"Yep. They're spies. Spies for Hollywood. I seen their type at conferences before. They get a job there just so as they can steal story ideas from writers and then sell 'em to the producers. They make big bucks, and us poor writers, working hard to come up with our own stuff, are left in the dirt. We go to the movies and find some movie mogul has stolen our ideas and put 'em up on the big screen. And we're left with nothin'. Absolutely nothin.'"

"These aren't spies, Mr. . . ."

"Jes' call me Walter. I ain't got no other name I care to share."

"Walter. I can guarantee these girls are not spies."

"But I heard 'em talking to a producer. Talked to 'im myself one day."

"They have a friend in the television business. He calls and pretends he's all kinds of people. It's a game. To make them laugh. He's very funny."

Walter stared at the girls. His face wrinkles surrounded the "O" of his mouth like a series of parentheses. He shuffled quickly away.

"Glenda," Mr. Kiersey said.

Glenda marched up to the front of the room, Rahja in tow. Anger played double time on her face. "Mr. Kiersey, I've kept my mouth shut long enough. But when I think a wrong is being committed, I can't stand by and do nothing."

Mr. Kiersey wiped his brow. "Can this one wait until tomorrow? There's an awful lot going on right now."

"No, it can't wait. An innocent, good worker is about to be replaced by these two impostors."

Mr. Kiersey's head dropped to one side. "Please, go on," he said in a monotone.

"I overheard Rahja telling the assistant manager that one worker was going to be replaced because she wasn't doing a good enough job. That her file showed she was under probation for possible stealing. I know

Lori didn't steal. Lori would never steal. Then these two show up and try to act real good and work real fast, and I know they are just here to take Lori's job. I even caught them with Lori's file, trying to add stuff to it that wasn't true. But Lori was sick with the flu for two days before she knew what was wrong, so she wasn't working her best. I don't think Rahja should fire her just for that, do you?"

Mr. Kiersey looked at Rahja, seeming to age years right before China's eyes. "It wasn't Lori you were going to fire, was it?"

Rahja shook his head and rubbed his dark beard. "I think Lori is one of the best workers we have. There is another worker who is permanently being replaced. But I did not think that was your business, Glenda."

"Besides," he said, "these two girls live here. They were only working because we needed the help. I thought I told you that."

Glenda looked at the floor. "I thought you said they were going to live here."

China looked at the ceiling and shook her head.

"I'm sorry for how I treated you," Glenda said to China and Deedee. Then she paused and asked, "Why were you in the file room?"

"YOU were in the file room?" Mr. Kiersey asked. "Here I was so worried about what information was taken from there. And it was only you. Why didn't you tell me?" After a moment's hesitation, he said. "Why *were* you there?"

Deedee looked at her hands. "We were looking for someone named Harrison, because we thought Belina was going to murder him. We thought he might be at this camp. And since no one would believe us . . ."

"Never mind," Mr. Kiersey said, rubbing his temples. "Everyone can leave now."

"What about us?" asked the reporter from the *Star World Enterprise* tabloid.

Mr. Kiersey raised his eyebrows at the girls.

"We thought you were B.T. playing a joke on us," China told him.

"We're sorry," Deedee added.

The reporter looked at them. "We can still have an interview, can't we?"

"About what?" asked Deedee.

"I want to know all about B.T. What he's really like. What he looks like in a swimsuit. What he likes in a girl." He raised his eyebrow at the last statement.

"Sorry," Deedee said.

"He's a friend," China told him. "We'd never talk about a friend to the press."

The reporter looked very disappointed. "But we pay an awful lot of money."

The girls shook their heads. "Don't even try," China said.

"We're not interested," Deedee said.

"I can't go home empty-handed," he said.

"There's a room full of writers," China said. "I bet they've got lots of stories to tell."

❧

"We're never going to live this down, China," Deedee said, as they walked home through the forest.

China smiled. "Yeah. But at least I leave here at the
end of summer. You have to live with it the rest of
your entire life."

"You have always been such an encouragement to
me," Deedee said sarcastically. She moved around a
large rock blocking their way.

"I'm surprised your dad let us loose. I thought he'd
have us under lock and key and alarm for the next
few days."

"Or at least take us to the infirmary to get our ears
cleaned out."

They both laughed.

"Dad's going to ask us what lesson we learned from
all this."

China sighed. "Oh great. Another meeting with the
big boss. I like your dad much better when he's just a
dad."

"So? What are we going to tell him?"

"That we will never have important discussions
while ripping someone off the Velcro wall."

Deedee raised her eyebrows. "That was it, wasn't it?
And the telephone at the ranch."

"And the noise of the kitchen. It seemed like every
time we talked about writers something happened."

"Not *every* time. But maybe once you get it into

your head that you've heard one thing, it kind of sticks there."

China tilted her head back and opened her arms to the cool evening. "I know one thing. Eavesdropping will no longer be a reliable source of information for me."

"I like that. Remember how you said that. Dad would like that a lot."

After they crossed the creek, Deedee shook out her hair like a wild woman. When she came up for air, she remembered the television producer. "What about Mr. Gleckenspiel?"

"I say we give the man a call. Tonight."

"But we don't have B.T.'s phone number."

China munched her lips together. "That is a slight problem."

The minute they walked through the screen door, the phone rang. It was B.T. "At least one thing has gone right today," China whispered to Deedee before they got on separate phones.

"Samuel J. Gleckenspiel said you acted real strange on the phone today," B.T. said. "He asked me to call you and see if everything is okay."

"Don't be funny, B.T.," China said. "We know it was you."

"No it wasn't."

"B.T., tell us the truth."

"I am. Honest."

"You're going to have to prove it," Deedee said.

"We've had too many misunderstandings and stuff going on."

"Tell papa all about it," B.T. said in an old man's voice.

"I don't know . . ." Deedee started.

"We might as well," China said. "He'll probably hear it from someone else anyway. I wouldn't be surprised if we make front page on the *Star World Enterprise* tabloid next week."

"Excuse me?" B.T. said. "Now you *have* to tell me."

They told the story, both girls interjecting different parts until B.T. was rolling on the floor laughing.

"If you don't stop that," China warned, "we won't finish the story."

Between guffaws, B.T. could hardly get out, "You can't be serious. You guys are worse than I am!"

"Can you see why we don't think Mr. Samuel J. is real?" Deedee asked.

"Okay. To prove it he wants to take you girls to lunch and have a tour of the camp on Saturday. I can't come, but he'll have all his identification with him."

China felt her heart leap to her throat. She swallowed hard. *Meeting a Hollywood producer? I don't know if I can handle this.*

B.T. hung up since he couldn't get much out of the two speechless girls.

China hardly knew how she got ready for bed. Exhaustion and shock had finally taken over. Once in bed, she said, "Deedee. I've been thinking. God answered our prayers. Harrison didn't die."

"He only broke his foot," Deedee mumbled, fast on her way to internal lights out.

"Can we sleep through next week?" China asked, rolling over on her sleeping bag.

"Can't. We have to be Tribal Village leaders next week. The flu's struck there now."

"Good . . . little kids. Nothing can go wrong there, right?"

"Don't say that China."

"What should I say?"

"Goodnight."

"Goodnight."

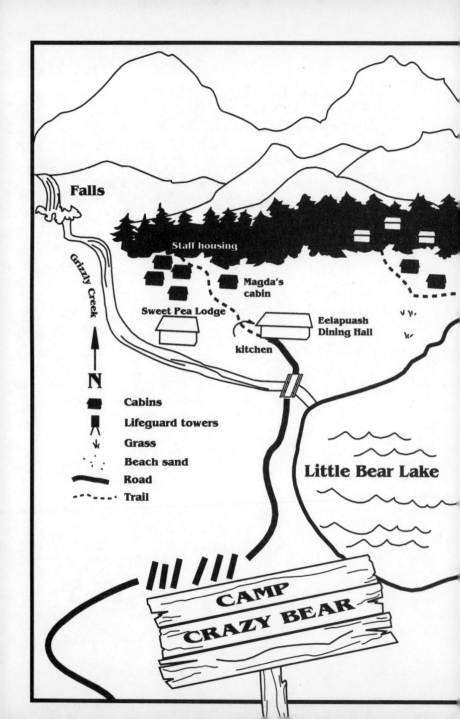

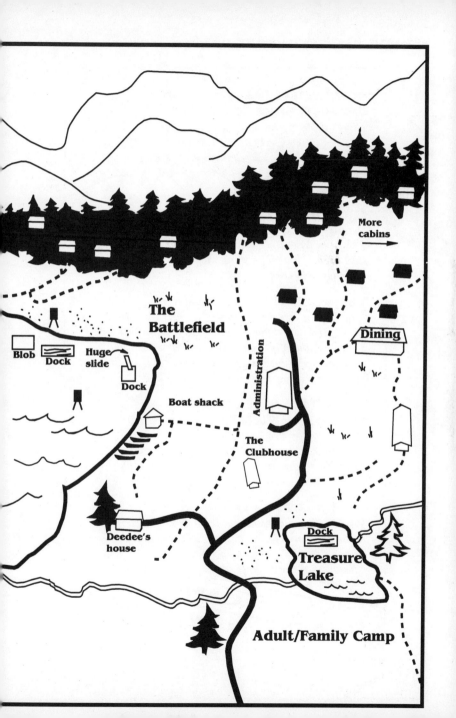

Brio

Designed especially for teen girls, Brio *is packed with super stories, intriguing interviews and amusing articles on the topics they care about most—relationships, fitness, fashion and more—all from a Christian perspective.*

All magazines are published monthly except where otherwise noted. For more information regarding these and other resources, please call Focus on the Family, at (719) 531-5181, or write to us at Focus on the Family, Colorado Springs, CO 80995.